"Travis?"

Chelsea's heart poun[...] [...] [...] felt a little
foolish, but the fear pushed her forward.

He turned.

"Would you mind staying with me tonight? I'm
embarrassed to admit it but I'm still a little shaky."

"You have nothing to be embarrassed about," he
said, heading back to the bed.

She scooted over to make room for him. He toed off
his shoes and slid in beside her still in his clothes.

She relaxed against him.

He wrapped an arm around her waist and he
gathered her close. The faint smell of his cologne still
lingered even after the night they'd had.

"I feel safe when I'm with you."

"I'm glad I make you feel safe."

His breath tickled the skin on her neck, causing her
pulse to pick up. She'd meant it when she'd asked
him to only sleep next to her, but her body didn't
seem to want to cooperate with her. Lying next to him
was sweet torture.

THE PERFECT MURDER

K.D. RICHARDS

Harlequin

INTRIGUE

Harlequin®
INTRIGUE™

ISBN-13: 978-1-335-45705-9

The Perfect Murder

Copyright © 2024 by Kia Dennis

Recycling programs for this product may not exist in your area.

For questions and comments about the quality of this book, please contact us at CustomerService@Harlequin.com.

TM and ® are trademarks of Harlequin Enterprises ULC.

 Harlequin Enterprises ULC
22 Adelaide St. West, 41st Floor
Toronto, Ontario M5H 4E3, Canada
www.Harlequin.com

Printed in Lithuania

MIX
Paper | Supporting responsible forestry
FSC® C021394

K.D. Richards is a native of the Washington, DC, area, who now lives outside Toronto with her husband and two sons. You can find her at kdrichardsbooks.com.

Books by K.D. Richards

Harlequin Intrigue

West Investigations

Pursuit of the Truth
Missing at Christmas
Christmas Data Breach
Shielding Her Son
Dark Water Disappearance
Catching the Carling Lake Killer
Under the Cover of Darkness
A Stalker's Prey
Silenced Witness
Lakeside Secrets
The Perfect Murder

Visit the Author Profile page at Harlequin.com.

CAST OF CHARACTERS

Chelsea Harper—A teacher investigating the wrongful conviction of her father.

Travis Collins—West Investigations private detective and former police officer.

Franklin Brooks—Chelsea's father, convicted of a crime he didn't commit.

Gabe Owens—Travis's friend and a police detective.

Victor Thompson—Chelsea's cousin and best friend.

Brenda Thompson—Chelsea's aunt.

Bill Rowland—Franklin Brooks's best friend.

Chapter One

He'd worried for years waiting for Franklin Brooks to exhaust all of his appeals. And now the last appeal was over, and he should be able to relax, confident that another man would be paying for the crime he'd committed. But he couldn't relax. Because Chelsea just wouldn't let it go.

He couldn't believe Chelsea Harper, a third-grade teacher, had the skills to hack into the LAPD's computer system, but whoever she'd gotten to do it had been good. If he hadn't had the foresight to flag Lily Wong's case file, he would have never known it had been accessed and downloaded remotely. The hacker hadn't left a trail, either. Thank goodness he'd been notified the moment the file was accessed. Knowing about the hack while it was happening was the only reason he'd been able to follow it back to its source. After that it had been easy to search through the hacker's computer and find out who'd hired him to steal Lily's file.

He hadn't meant to kill her. His precious Lily. He'd tried to make her understand they were meant to be together. She wouldn't listen.

Killing her had been an accident. His rage had exploded, and before he realized it, she was dead.

Franklin getting blamed for it had been a fluke. A convenient fluke.

He hadn't had to run. He hadn't had to leave his life.

But if Chelsea Harper succeeded in her quest to clear her father's name, he might have to now.

No. No, he wouldn't let her destroy his life.

He finished his breakfast, loading his dishes into the dishwasher and straightening the kitchen before he prepared to leave for work. Years of monotonous, solitary drudgery among boxes and in dark rooms had given him a superpower. Invisibility. It would come in handy. He'd need to keep an eye on Chelsea. And, if he had to, deal with her the same way he'd dealt with Lily.

Chapter Two

Chelsea Harper paused for a moment just inside the West Security and Investigations West Coast offices. The private investigations firm was located in a single-story brick building in West Hollywood. She passed through double glass doors into a small lobby where an attractive twenty-something Latina woman typed on a computer behind the reception desk. The decor was sleek and masculine with dark leather sofas and an uninspired snapshot of the iconic Hollywood sign on the white wall.

"Hello," she said, giving the receptionist, whose name plate read Bailey Lee, a smile. "I'd like to speak with Travis Collins, please."

Bailey returned her smile with one that looked genuine. She tapped a few keys, her smile slightly dimming when her gaze returned to Chelsea's face. "Is Mr. Collins expecting you?"

"No." Chelsea bit her bottom lip. She had considered calling to make an appointment, but she'd been afraid that Travis Collins would refuse to see her, so she'd opted for an ambush instead. "But I'm hoping he can make time for me."

"And your name is?" Bailey asked, reaching for the phone receiver.

"Chelsea Harper."

Bailey spoke quietly into the receiver for a moment. "Mr. Collins will be right out. You can have a seat while you wait if you'd like." She motioned to the leather sofas with one hand and reset the phone receiver with the other.

Chelsea was too nervous to sit. She backed away from the receptionist's desk but stayed standing. She examined the photos on the wall, not really seeing them. For maybe the hundredth time, she wondered if she was doing the right thing bringing on an investigator. Especially this particular investigator. For a second, she considered turning around and leaving, but Travis Collins rounded the corner before she could make a break for it.

She'd seen him on the news and had read several online articles that mentioned him while she was investigating PIs, so she knew he was thirty-five years old and an attractive man. Real-life Travis Collins was not just attractive, he was impressively masculine. He was tall and lean and wearing a suit that fit him like he had been born in it. His short, cropped hair was shot through with the beginning of gray. He moved toward her with a stride that was both confident and noble. His dark brown eyes fell on her face, and she watched as he quickly sized her up from head to toe.

His gaze met hers as he approached, and she saw the moment he recognized her. It had been a long time since anyone recognized her like that, but she wasn't surprised that he had. Her face had been in the papers almost as much as her father's during his trial, reporters hounding her to no end. And Travis was a detective and a private investigator, trained to remember details.

"Chelsea Brooks?" His expression was a cross between surprise and shock.

"It's Chelsea Harper now."

"You got married?"

She shook her head. "I took my aunt and uncle's last name after…" The press and social media had made it impossible to keep her father's name even during the years she'd lived in San Francisco immediately after college.

He nodded. "I understand."

She doubted that he did but kept that thought to herself.

"What can I do for you?"

"I'd like to hire you."

One of his eyebrows cocked upward. "Hire me?"

"Yes. I understand you have left the LAPD and are a private investigator now." She waved a hand vaguely to encompass the lobby. "I want to hire you to help me prove my father's innocence."

His brow came down now as his eyes narrowed suspiciously. "Let's go into a conference room. We can talk more freely there."

He led her down a hallway to a small glass-walled conference room. She took a seat at the large round table, and he offered her coffee and water, which she declined. She was too anxious to drink.

Travis sat across from her at the table. He looked like he wasn't sure how to start the conversation. Finally, he said, "Why don't you tell me exactly what you're hoping West Investigations can do for you?"

She cocked her head to the side. "As you know, my father was convicted of the murder of Lily Wong, his former girlfriend."

Of course he knew. He had not been involved in her father's case, but he had been on the force, and Lily's murder was big news for more than a year. Chelsea knew it might seem odd for her to seek his help in proving her father's innocence. She'd spent countless hours debating whether he was the right man for the job. But West Security and Investigations was one of the best PI firms on either coast, and in the years since her father had been convicted, Travis had proved he was willing to go up against the system in general and the LAPD in particular to do the right thing. She was going to need that kind of courage and conviction if she had any hope of winning her father's freedom.

"He's exhausted all his appeals. The only way to get him out of jail now is to prove he was wrongly convicted."

Travis's expression remained sympathetic. "These past seven years must have been hard for you," he started.

"You have no idea, Mr. Collins."

"Call me Travis, please."

"Travis. And you can call me Chelsea. Travis, my father is innocent. He did not kill Lily Wong."

She watched him stiffen in his chair. "Ms. Harper—"

She held up a hand, stopping him. "I'm sure you heard that a lot as a police detective, but you're not a cop now, so I hope you'll hear me out."

He hesitated before nodding that she should continue.

"My father has always maintained his innocence. In the years since his trial, I've gathered as much information as I could, news articles, police reports, whatever I could get my hands on, and I've pored over them." She wasn't sure how he would react to the conclusions she'd drawn from her review of the police investigation, but if there was any chance of them working together, it was best to get everything out in the open now. "Frankly, the police investigation was lacking. They homed in on my dad and never looked at anyone else."

The look he gave her was one of disbelief. "It may seem that way to you, but a jury convicted your father."

"Based on the limited evidence collected by the cops and presented by the prosecutor," she responded fiercely.

"Ms. Harper, I know we are talking about your father. I'm sure you love him, but I don't have time—"

"I'm not here to waste your time, Mr. Collins," she interjected sharply. "I'm here to hire you. I want to clear my father's name and get him out of prison. But more than that, I want Lily's real murderer to pay. Whoever killed her has gotten away with the crime for all these years. My dad wants to rectify that." She paused for a moment before adding quietly. "And my dad wasn't the only one who cared about Lily."

"Chelsea, it has been seven years. I wouldn't even know where to begin."

He may have thought that statement would deter her, but it showed he was thinking about where to begin. A good sign in her book. "There are discrepancies in the witness statements." She reached into her handbag and pulled out a crinkled letter-size envelope. "My aunt received this note last week. I think the witness who placed my dad at Lily's house, Peter Schmeichel—"

Travis gave her a look that drew a smile from her along with a shrug.

"Hey, I didn't name him. Take it up with his parents. As I was saying, I think the witness who placed my dad at Lily's house perjured himself on the witness stand."

She handed him the letter and envelope and watched as he read it once, then once more. She knew the words by heart.

Peter Schmeichel lied. He didn't see your brother at the dead girl's house that night.

Travis shook his head. She was losing him. "This isn't evidence." He turned the envelope over, looking, she was sure, for a return address or some indication where it might have come from. There was nothing but a postage stamp indicating it had been mailed from California. No help.

"I know." She nearly growled the words. "The police detective I took it to all but laughed at me and the prosecutor wouldn't even meet with me. But if it's true—"

He cut her off. "If, and that's a very big if. We don't even know who sent this." He held up the note.

She didn't need to hear the suspicion in his voice to know what he was getting at. "You think my father, or I, sent the note. To what end? If I could get anyone to believe me, they'd just go find Peter, and he'd stick to his story. What would sending the note to myself get me or my dad in the end?"

Suspicion still clouded his face, but he said, "I'm willing to concede that it makes no sense for you or your dad to send the note, but that doesn't make the note true."

"But it's worth looking into. It might be my father's only chance." She hated the pleading tone of her voice, but if pleading was what it took to get him to help her, she'd do it. She reached out and took his hand in both of hers. His brown skin was smooth, and she couldn't help noticing how perfectly her hand fit with his. "Please. Please. Just come with me to visit my father tomorrow at the prison. Listen to his story. If you still don't believe him, I'll never bother you again."

The expression on his face was inscrutable.

She took her hand back. "At the very least you'll get paid for a day's work."

"One day. That's all I can promise you."

"And you listen with an open mind," she countered.

"And I'll listen with an open mind," he agreed.

The tension she had been carrying inside of her eased. Over the first hurdle and only hundreds more to go.

"If you give me your contact information, I will have the paperwork emailed to you. You can read it and sign it tonight and give it to me tomorrow. What time are we expected at Chino?" he asked, referencing the California Institution for Men by its common nickname.

Chelsea nodded. "Yes. Visiting hours start at eleven."

"I'll pick you up at your place at ten then. Let me walk you out."

He walked her to the entrance and shook her hand before she pushed out into the Los Angeles heat. She could feel his eyes still on her as she stepped off the curb. She was in the middle of the street when the roar of an engine came from her right. She froze as a black sedan careened toward her. Seconds passed as she processed the moment. Then her brain finally sent the message to her feet to move.

She leaped for the opposite curb. A sharp pain whipped through her hip right before she hit the pavement and rolled between two parked cars.

It felt as if the pain was coming from everywhere. She struggled to take in a breath.

Then Travis Collins's face appeared, hovering over hers. "Chelsea? Are you okay?" His voice sounded as if it was coming from a distance even though he was centimeters away.

She wasn't sure how to answer that. She struggled to push herself up into a sitting position, but gentle hands held her down.

"Don't move. An ambulance is on its way." He lifted her head gently and rested it on his knees.

"I don't need an ambulance."

"You were clipped by a car. You definitely need to be checked out at the hospital."

Sirens wailed in the distance. A man in a suit jogged to Travis's side. "I tried to catch him, but he got away."

"Did you get a look at the license plate?" Travis asked the man.

The man was hunched over, hands on his knees, trying to catch his breath, but he shook his head. "Sorry, dude. The guy must have been drunk or something."

"That was no drunk driver," Travis said, looking down at Chelsea, his gaze serious. "I think someone just tried to kill you."

Chapter Three

Travis rode with Chelsea in the ambulance to the hospital and didn't leave her side while the doctor checked her over. She was lucky. She had a few bruises and a deep gash on her arm that needed a handful of stitches, but she had no broken bones or permanent damage. She sat on a gurney in the curtained area of the emergency room, clutching Travis's hand in a death grip while the doctor stitched her arm.

The day had taken a very unexpected turn. He had planned to wrap up his current case, a fraud investigation for an insurance client who suspected a business owner of faking a series of thefts from his store. Travis had caught the owner on camera taking stock that had supposedly been stolen from the store from a self-storage locker and selling it out of his home. He'd already forwarded the photos to his client, but he needed to put the finishing touches on his report. That had been the plan for the day before Chelsea Harper walked into the West offices.

Chelsea squeezed his hand, and he glanced down at her face. He could tell she was trying to hide it, but she was in pain. That thought sent a bubble of anger rising in his chest.

Over her shoulders, he saw the automatic doors to the

emergency room open. Kevin Lombard, his boss and West Security and Investigations' operations manager, strode in with Tess Stenning, head of the West Coast office.

He gave Chelsea's hand a squeeze and rose. "I'll be right back."

Chelsea clutched his hand. "Don't leave me?"

"Of course not. I'm just going to talk to my boss. Right over there." He jerked his head to where Tess and Kevin waited for him.

He could feel Chelsea's eyes following him as he crossed the emergency room.

"How is she?" Kevin asked. Like Travis, Kevin was a former cop who had signed on with West Security and Investigations when the firm opened up its West Coast office.

"Okay. She had a gash on her arm that required stitches, but otherwise she was unharmed."

"That's a relief," Tess said. "I don't know how I would have explained to Ryan and Sean if a client got seriously injured right outside our offices." Although Tess was the head of West Security and Investigations West Coast division, she reported to Sean and Ryan West, the co-owners who remained in the firm's New York headquarters.

"Were you able to get any info from witnesses about the car or driver?" Travis asked. He'd given Tess a quick description of the hit and run before leaving for the hospital with Chelsea.

Tess shook her head. "Nothing. But we're working on getting security footage from the surrounding businesses. Unfortunately, the angle wasn't good enough to get a clear shot from our own cameras."

"Someone knew Chelsea was coming to see me. This wasn't an accident."

Tess nodded. "That or they were following her, but either way I agree this doesn't look like an accident."

"Do you think it was a warning or..." Kevin let the rest of the sentence hang.

Travis shook his head, his rage barely contained. "I don't know, but you better believe I intend to find out." His jaw clenched, and a hot rage bubbled in his gut. "Let me know when you get that security footage from the nearby businesses."

There was no reason for him to feel so protective of Chelsea—he barely knew her—but he did.

"Already on it," Kevin responded.

Tess gave Travis a searching look. "Bailey said Ms. Harper came in without an appointment and asked for you specifically. Do you two know each other?"

"Yes and no. She's Franklin Brooks's daughter. I wasn't involved in the case, but he was convicted seven years ago for killing his former girlfriend."

"And why did Ms. Harper want to speak with you?" Tess pressed.

"She wants to hire West Investigations to prove her father's innocence."

"Wait." Kevin held up a hand. "You said her father has already been convicted."

Travis sighed. "He was, but he never stopped professing his innocence. He's exhausted his appeals, but Chelsea says she's found evidence that a key witness may have lied at his trial."

Both frowns deepened.

"Okay," Kevin said. "That's all fine and good, but her father has been convicted and his appeal denied. I don't see how we can help."

Travis held his hands up, hoping to ward off his bosses'

arguments. "Hey, I know what it sounds like. So does Chelsea. She's asked me to meet with her father tomorrow, and I've agreed." He held a hand up higher stopping the oncoming protest. "I've made it clear to her that's all I'm agreeing to. One meeting. I'll hear Franklin Brooks out, but I've promised nothing."

Tess and Kevin groaned.

"I know. I felt the same way. Until the hit-and-run," Travis responded pointedly.

"The two things may not be related," Tess countered.

Travis shot her a look.

She shrugged. "I said they may not be related."

"Unlikely." Travis ran a hand over his head. "Chelsea comes to me about proving her father's innocence, and she's not ten steps from the office when someone tries to run her down? Something is going on here whether Franklin Brooks is innocent or guilty."

"And she's willing to pay our fee for this investigation?" Tess, ever the businesswoman, asked. "It may be a lot of expense for nothing."

"I'm not going to lead her on. One day. Limited expense, then I'll let her down as gently as possible." He thought about Chelsea having to take her uncle's name just to get away from the press, and anger bubbled. Whatever her father had done, she didn't deserve to be punished for it.

"You know digging into this could put you at odds with your friends at the LAPD, right?" Tess stated the obvious.

Travis frowned. "I doubt very much anyone at the LAPD considers themselves my friend. At least not anymore. And if, and I know it's a very big if, Chelsea is right, I want to make it right."

"I don't know how much of her father's story is true, but

the lady has definitely acquired an enemy," Kevin said, shooting a glance at the bed where Chelsea was still getting stitched up. "There is one thing we should consider." Kevin hesitated before continuing, "Chelsea could have set this up herself. Hired someone to drive that car at her."

The look on Tess's face said she'd thought of this as well.

Chelsea's fear-filled brown eyes popped into Travis's head, and he instinctively rejected the idea. "You didn't see her face when she was lying there in the street. She was stunned and terrified. She didn't do that to herself." He glanced over his shoulder to where Chelsea lay on the rolling bed alone now, the doctor having finished her stitches. He turned back to his colleagues in time to catch them sharing a look. "What?"

"Do you think you might be too close to this to be objective?" Tess asked.

"No," he answered quickly. Maybe too quickly. "Look, do I feel sorry for her? Yes. She was twenty-two years old when her father was convicted. The local media around this was not kind to her. She had to take her aunt and uncle's last name to get away from it. But every convict professes their innocence. Franklin Brooks is guilty."

"But…" Kevin cocked an eyebrow.

"But something is going on here, and my gut tells me Chelsea might have put herself in real danger."

Tess shook her head. "Not another one. I'm surrounded by knights in shining armor."

He was no knight. But he was convinced something dangerous was going on, and he was going to find out what it was.

TRAVIS DROVE CHELSEA home after taking her to have the prescription the doctor had given her filled. He had sug-

gested she call someone to come stay with her. She'd told
him she would consider it, but she really just wanted to be
alone. Still, she did leave a message for her cousin Victor, telling him she'd had a minor run-in with a car but
that she was okay and resting at home. She was sure she'd
have to answer for that less-than-descriptive message but
hoped it would wait until tomorrow.

She swallowed two of the pills the doctor had pre-
scribed and made a large bowl of popcorn for dinner. She
usually loved to cook, but she didn't have the energy tonight, nor a taste for takeout.

When the popcorn was ready, she carried it and a large
glass of water (since alcohol and painkillers didn't mix)
to the sofa and flipped through the movie channels. *Bat-
man*, the one with Michael Keaton, was on, and she'd just
settled in to watch when the sound of the front door click-
ing open drew her attention.

Only Victor and her aunt Brenda had keys to her house,
so she wasn't surprised when her cousin appeared in the
doorway between the kitchen and family room a moment
later.

"Chelsea Antoinette Harper, are you okay?"

"I'm fine, Victor. I told you that in my message," she
said, moving the blanket covering her legs to the side and
starting to rise.

"Do not get up." Victor marched across the room and
sat next to her on the sofa. Gently, he pulled her into his
arms and gave her a sideways hug. "I can't believe you
didn't call me."

"I knew you were at work."

Victor was a teacher just like her, but he had elected to
teach summer school. Chelsea usually did, too, but she'd

planned to devote this summer to doing everything she could to finally free her father.

"I would have dropped everything if I'd known you needed me. You know that."

"I do. But like I said, I'm fine, and I wasn't alone."

Victor's eyebrows went up.

"The private investigator I hired was with me."

"Private investigator?"

"Yes. I hired him to help me with my father's case. I've done a lot by myself, but I think I could use some professional help."

"Chelsea—"

"I know you think I should just get on with my life, but—"

"It's not that I don't believe in Uncle Franklin's innocence," Victor started. He had taken a more measured approach to her father's predicament than his mother, who wanted nothing to do with her older brother, but Chelsea knew Victor had his doubts. He'd never laid them all out for her, preferring to remain Switzerland between Chelsea and Brenda.

"I get it, Victor, I do."

"I'm just worried about you. You said you were at the hospital with your private investigator. Was he with you when you got hit?"

"I was leaving his office. He was inside, but he saw it."

"Does he think the hit-and-run is connected to your investigation?"

"I'm sure it isn't," she lied.

"Uh-huh."

"Are you going to do something pedestrian, like order me to stop investigating?"

"You know me well enough to know I would never do anything pedestrian. I am worried about you, though."

"Don't be."

"Oh, don't be. Well, poof, I'm no longer worried. You know it doesn't work that way. You're family."

"So is my dad."

"I'm not saying he's not…"

"I know, and I know you don't mean anything by it, but I can't drop this."

"Do you really think you can turn up something the police didn't? Even after seven years?"

"I don't know," she said, exasperated. "Maybe not. But I have to try everything I possibly can to get my father his life back."

Victor bumped her shoulder with his. "You're amazing, you know that?"

"Well…" Chelsea flipped her hair over one shoulder and vamped.

"And so humble, too." Victor tossed a piece of popcorn at her. "By the way, this—" he circled the popcorn bowl with his index finger "—does not qualify as dinner. I'm going to call Novita's. Do you want me to order something for you?"

Chelsea sighed inside. It looked like she wasn't going to get her quiet, restful night at home, after all.

Chapter Four

Travis suggested rescheduling their appointment to meet with Franklin Brooks, but Chelsea insisted they keep it. If they missed their prearranged visitation time, it would be at least another week, probably considerably longer, before Chelsea could get set up another time to visit her father.

Travis had taken her home after her discharge from the hospital and promised to return the next morning at ten to take her to the prison. When she opened her front door to him that morning, she only looked slightly more rested than when he dropped her off the day before. But she grabbed her purse and locked the front door to the house, ignoring his renewed suggestion of putting off the visit.

It was a forty-minute drive to Chino. They passed the time with pleasantries. Chelsea told him all about her plans for her third-grade class in the fall. It was clear she was a passionate and engaged teacher, dedicated to doing her best for each of the kids who passed through her classroom doors. He wasn't surprised, given how zealously she was championing her father's cause.

The prison was a blocky, red-brick, one-story structure. A high fence topped with razor wire wound around the perimeter. Travis drove through the main gate and to the visitors' parking lot. He parked the car, then led Chelsea into the prison.

Prisons always felt like...well, prisons. The air was thick with the smell of disinfectant and despair. It hit him the moment he walked in. He and Chelsea got in line behind another family queued up to sign in and go through the series of indignities required in order to see their incarcerated family member or friend. The guards at the desk were efficient, checking names on driver's licenses against the names on the list of visitors allowed inside, then waving each person on to the lockers.

Travis and Chelsea showed their identification and stored their personal items—his wallet and her purse—in a locker before going through a set of metal detectors. After lining up again, they were led along with the other visitors to a large cream-colored room.

Fluorescent lights flickered overhead, and a half-dozen cafeteria tables lined the walls on either side of the room. The visitors trampled down the middle aisle, claiming seats at various tables. A mechanical buzzing echoed through the room after they were all seated.

Prisoners clad in drab gray jumpsuits, with Department of Corrections and their prisoner numbers penned on the left side of their chests, shuffled into the room.

Franklin Brooks was one of the last men to enter. He had aged quite a bit in the seven years since Travis had last seen him. His dark brown dreads had gone mostly gray. He'd lost weight but gained muscle. His skin was sallow, and his eyes were hooded, undoubtedly from the horrors he'd seen behind bars. But his smile when his gaze landed on Chelsea was pure and filled with love.

"Hi, Daddy." Chelsea stepped into her father's arms.

Brooks's arms tightened around his daughter, and his

eyes closed. The hug went on long enough to draw a cough and a frown from a nearby prison guard.

The prison had strict rules about touching. Brief touches such as hugs and handshakes were allowed at the beginning and end of visitation hour.

Brooks pulled away, his gaze moving to Travis. His smile fell into something more akin to a grimace. "Mr. Collins, thanks for coming."

Travis took Brooks's outstretched hand and shook it briefly. Travis sat next to Chelsea on one side of the table, and Brooks sat across from them on the other side.

"I wasn't sure Chelsea would be able to convince you to come see me, but I should have never doubted my girl." He smiled across the table at Chelsea.

Chelsea reached for her father's hand, giving it a quick squeeze before pulling back. "Travis has agreed to hear you out before he decides whether to help me investigate."

Travis frowned. He still had no intention of taking on investigating Franklin Brooks's case. As far as he was concerned, the justice system had spoken. He was more inclined toward investigating who had attempted to hit Chelsea.

"It would be best if you went over the details of your case. Starting at the beginning."

"The beginning," Brooks said acidly. "I'm not sure where that is, but I'll try." He took a deep breath and let it out slowly. "I wasn't a good father."

"Daddy—" Chelsea reached across the table for her father's hands.

"No, sweetheart. I wasn't." Brooks gave her hands a quick squeeze before pulling back. "If it wasn't for your aunt Brenda and uncle Darren taking us in and doing the lion's share of rearing you, I don't know where we would have been." His gaze went back to Travis's face. "Brenda is my sister. She and her husband took care of Chelsea like she was their own. Making sure she did her homework. Had clean clothes. Stayed away from the wrong crowds when she was a teen. She acted as Chelsea's parent after her mother died and while I drank too much, too often. Catted around with women when I should have been home, raising my daughter. I'm ashamed to say I never really grew up. At least not until I got here." He motioned to the prison walls. "And didn't have a choice."

Travis hadn't traveled all the way to Chino to hold a therapy session with Brooks. If the man was feeling remorse over how he'd lived his life, he was sorry, but he wasn't a therapist. "I understand," he said, nodding for Brooks to go on.

Brooks smiled knowingly. "Yes, of course. I don't want you to think I'm wasting your time, Mr. Collins. I just want you to understand what our life was like back when—"

Travis tapped into his store of patience. "When Lily Wong was killed."

Brooks glanced at Chelsea who nodded her encouragement. "Yes. Like I said, I dated a lot of women back then, but Lily was different. I loved her."

"How did you meet Lily?"

Brooks smiled, his eyes going glassy as if he was remembering. "At the park. She'd gone to a yoga class, and when she got back to her car, it wouldn't start. She called the garage where I worked, and I was sent out with the tow truck to see if I could get her car started. I couldn't. I had to tow it in, and by the time we got back to the shop, I had a date for the weekend."

"So, you two hit it off right away?" Travis asked.

"Right away. She was just so beautiful and so fun. And

funny, a real quick wit. Everybody loved being around her. You remember, don't you, Chels?"

"I do." Chelsea grinned. "She always made me laugh."

Brooks laughed then, too. "Always."

"When did the relationship start to sour?" That was one thing Travis remembered clearly from the trial. As good as things may have been between Franklin and Lily at the beginning of their relationship, it definitely hadn't been good around the time of Lily's murder.

Brooks's face fell. "When my drinking picked up. I'll be the first to admit it got out of hand. I've been in AA since I got to this lovely establishment. But it took me a long time to admit I had a problem."

"What happened the day Lily was killed?" Travis asked, getting to the reason he was there. It hadn't been his case and he only remembered bits and pieces of the news reports that had come out about Lily's murder and Franklin's conviction. And it was always best to hear a story directly from the source.

Brooks let out a sigh. "I've gone over it hundreds, thousands of times in my head. I convinced Lily to meet me at Billiards, a bar we like to go to. She had broken things off with me about a month earlier, sick of my drinking. And yes, my cheating on her. I had been trying to get her back. Cleaning up my act and proving to her that I could be the man she deserved." Brooks paused, looking down at the table.

Chelsea shifted in her seat. It couldn't have been easy for her to hear her father talk about his faults, but her expression remained nonjudgmental.

"Lily and I had a couple drinks. We talked, but she wasn't buying that I had changed. She said she was through. She deserved better, and she'd moved on." Brooks's gaze rose. "She said she'd met someone new. I got angry. I yelled at her. Said horrible things. Things I didn't mean. She left the bar, and I followed her to her house."

"And then what happened?" Travis pressed. Visitation was only for an hour, and they were already nearing half an hour in. He wanted to make sure he got as much detail from Brooks as possible before he left.

"Lily wouldn't let me in her house. I can't say I blame her. I was angry. We argued some more on her front porch, and then I left. That's the last time I saw her. I swear. I went to another bar, I could never remember the name of it, just some dive, and drank myself stupid. I'm not sure when I left or how I got to the park where Lily and I met, but I know I woke up there in the parking lot the next morning with one helluva hangover. I went home, and I was sleeping it off when the cops showed up and took me in."

It was a story full of holes, which was probably why the lead detective had homed in on him in the first place. "And you have never been able to recall any specifics about what you did or where you went after leaving the bar? Not in the last seven years?" It didn't seem likely.

Brooks shook his head. "It's like the hours after I left Lily are just gone."

Travis's disbelief must have shown on his face.

Brooks's expression hardened. "Mr. Collins, I know you don't believe me."

"Your story is hard to believe."

Chelsea turned an angry gaze on Travis. "You said you would listen with an open mind."

"And I have. I just don't believe the story I'm hearing. Open mind or no."

Chelsea's cheeks mottled in anger. "What about the hit-

and-run? How do you explain that, or do you think it's just a coincidence that the very day I seek your help proving my father's innocence someone tries to run me down?"

"What?" Brooks's roar had most of the heads in the room turning in their direction.

Two of the guards headed toward them. "Keep it down, Brooks, or I will cut this party short," a beefy guard with a shaved head said in a gruff smoker's voice.

Brooks never took his gaze from his daughter. "What is this business about a hit-and-run?"

Chelsea's expression slipped from one of anger to one of chagrin. She clearly hadn't intended to tell her father about the hit-and-run, but the cat was out of the bag now. "I wasn't going to say anything. I didn't want to worry you." Her gaze slid from her father's face to the guards, who were still standing close by, and back to him nervously.

"Chelsea Antoinette Brooks. What is going on?"

Travis sat silently, watching the family drama play out.

"It's nothing to worry about. I was crossing the street yesterday when a car almost hit me. You know Los Angeles traffic. It was probably just some jerk racing off to an appointment."

Brooks held Chelsea's gaze for several long beats before turning to Travis. "You were there, yes?"

"It happened outside my agency's offices. I was inside the building, but I saw the whole thing from the window."

Brooks's eyes probed Travis's face. "Do you think it was just a drunk driving too fast and not paying attention?"

Travis could almost feel Chelsea willing him to say yes. But this was a father concerned about his daughter. If the roles were reversed, he would want the truth. So, he gave it to Brooks. "No, I don't. It looked like the driver was aiming for Chelsea."

Chelsea growled angrily next to him.

"I don't want you to investigate," Brooks said determinedly.

"Daddy—"

"Mr. Collins," Brooks said, looking Travis in the eye. "Thank you for coming out here today, but your services are no longer needed."

"It's not your decision to make," Chelsea ground out.

"It's my case and my life. That makes it my decision," Brooks shot back.

"It's my money," Chelsea countered.

The guards were looking their way again, and Travis didn't like the expressions on their faces. "Okay, let's just take a minute, and both of you cool down," he said. "I may not believe you, Brooks, but I don't not believe you, either. I don't know. The prosecutor's evidence against you was strong. But your sister recently received a note saying that Peter Schmeichel lied about seeing you at Lily's house around the time of her murder."

"Of course he lied. I may not be able to tell you exactly what I did after I left the bar that night, but I know—" Brooks pressed a fist over his heart "—in here that I didn't kill Lily."

"That's not going to be enough to get you out of jail," Travis responded.

"That's why I need your help," Chelsea countered.

"No," Brooks hissed. "I will not put you in danger."

Chelsea opened her mouth, but Travis spoke first. "It may be too late to avoid that."

"Then I want to hire you to protect Chelsea," Brooks said. "I don't know how much you charge, but I'll get it."

"Daddy, I don't need protection."

"Mr. Brooks, I'm not a bodyguard."

"You're a former cop. You served and protected for a living."

Chelsea slapped her hand on the table. "Is anyone listening to me? I don't need a bodyguard."

They had pushed the guards to their limit. The bald one came up behind Brooks. "All right, Brooks. That's enough. Time to go back to your cell."

Brooks didn't move.

Travis knew the situation could very easily and very quickly escalate. "I'll keep an eye on Chelsea," he said.

Beside him, another growl rumbled in Chelsea's throat.

Brooks's shoulders relaxed a fraction of an inch. "Thank you," he said, rising.

The guard put a hand on his shoulder and started turning him away, but Brooks resisted, looking at Chelsea. "Baby girl, be careful. You mean more to me than anything. Including my own life. I love you."

Brooks turned with the guard and let them lead him away then.

Chelsea fumed silently beside Travis while they collected their things and exited the prison. She didn't speak until they got to his car.

Travis opened the driver's-side door, but Chelsea glared at him over the car's hood. "What the hell was that?" she asked.

Travis sighed. He'd been asking himself the same question for the last several minutes, but he knew the answer. "That was me taking your case."

Chapter Five

Travis stood on Chelsea's welcome mat waiting for her to answer the door and wondering if he had made the right choice, agreeing to help her. Kevin hadn't been thrilled when Travis told him they were officially on the case. But something about Franklin Brooks's desperation to protect his daughter had gotten to Travis. That and the nagging suspicion that despite the evidence against her father, Chelsea might be onto something. When he'd dropped her off after leaving the prison, they'd agreed to meet up at her place later that evening to go over the files she'd collected.

Now the door opened, and Chelsea stood in front of him clad in yoga pants and a long-sleeve T-shirt, her feet bare. She'd put her hair atop her head in a messy bun from which curly tendrils fell to frame her heart-shaped face. The overall effect was sexy as hell.

"Hi," she said.

"Hey," he replied. "Can I come in?"

"Sorry. Yes, of course." She stepped back to allow him inside.

He followed her down a short hall, trying not to stare at her figure as he did, but it was hard not to. He'd always been attracted to curvy women, and Chelsea definitely had curves in all the right places. There was a grace to her that only came from being completely comfortable in her own skin. Her dark brown skin looked as if it had never seen a blemish, but it was her eyes that really pulled him in; violet-colored orbs that made him think of seduction.

He pulled his attention away from her and noticed that they had reached a living room, which opened up to the left, and a dining room was to the right. The dining room table was covered with boxes, and two big blue binders were stacked on top of one of them.

Chelsea paused in the entrance to the dining room. "This is my war room so to speak. Everything I have been able to find on my dad's case is in here."

"It seems like you've been able to get a lot."

"In some respects, yes. In others, not nearly enough." She began walking again, leading him to the kitchen at the back of the house. There was a second hall off the kitchen, and he could see three doors that opened onto it. Two bedrooms and a bathroom, he presumed. The house was small but cozy.

He sat on one of the two stools at the island counter. "What is all this?" He eyed the pots on the stove across from where he sat.

"I'm fixing us dinner. Beef shank ragù. I hope you like beef."

The smell had his stomach growling. He hadn't eaten since breakfast, and he suddenly realized he was ravenous. "I definitely do. But that sounds fancy."

Chelsea lifted the top of one of the pots and peeked inside. Obviously satisfied with what she saw, she placed the top back on. "Just a few more minutes. And it's really not that fancy. The pressure cooker does most of the work. I'm just cooking the pasta now. I figured we could eat and then get started going through the files."

"That works for me."

She smiled. "Great. Can I offer you something to drink? Water. Soda pop. Wine. I've also got beer."

"Beer for me, please."

"Is Corona okay?"

"Fine."

Chelsea pulled two bottles of Corona from the fridge and opened them both before sliding one his way.

He was glad she seemed to have gotten over her anger at him from that morning. It would definitely be easier to work together. He took a sip before speaking again. "So, I take it you like to cook?"

"Yeah." She took a pull from her bottle. "I find it relaxing. My aunt is an amazing cook, and I learned a lot from her. When I moved out on my own after college, I didn't want to get into the habit of eating out all the time. Not that I could afford to. How about you?"

"Do you mean do I cook? No. Not really." There were a handful of things he could make, but nothing like what she was talking about. "I'm pretty good at breakfast foods. Pancakes. Waffles. Even French toast, but nothing approaching beef shank ragù. I'm not even sure what a ragù is. Assuming we aren't talking about Chef Boyardee."

She laughed, and he felt warmth spread through his chest and limbs. "No. Definitely not. A ragù is basically just a meat-based sauce. The meat is braised and cooked in the sauce slowly over several hours. It's common for it to be served over pasta."

"So fancy spaghetti and meat sauce."

"Fancy spaghetti—" She fisted her hands on her hips, but her eyes sparkled, so he knew he hadn't actually offended her. "Go sit at the table." She pointed to the round table in the kitchen. "I'll show you fancy spaghetti." She laughed again, a slow sexy turnup of her mouth that sent a jolt through him. This felt a lot like flirting, something he did not do with clients.

Not that he didn't date. He did, usually quite regularly, although he'd been in a slump for the last several months. What he didn't do was relationships. Too messy, too likely that someone would get attached.

He never wanted to feel the pain of losing someone he loved again. The car accident that had taken the lives of his parents and his older brother, and had nearly taken his own when he was only ten, had left a wound that he wasn't sure would ever heal. He didn't think he could live through losing the woman he loved, and he was going to do everything he could not to ever put himself in that situation.

Maybe it was time to call one of his friends with benefits who understood that he was not looking for anything more than a pleasant weekend between two consenting adults. He'd been working a lot lately, so maybe after he put this case to bed, he'd take some time off. Maybe take a trip to Las Vegas or even splurge and fly to Hawaii. He lived frugally, so he could afford it.

He glanced at Chelsea, wondering if she'd ever been to Hawaii. He was positive she looked fabulous in a bikini. His groin tightened, and he shook the mental image from his head. She was a client, he reminded himself.

"Do you mind if I wash up before we eat?" he said, feeling the need to put a bit of distance between himself and Chelsea.

"Oh, sure. The bathroom is just down the hall." She pointed to the hall off the kitchen, confirming his earlier guess. "Second door to the left."

The bathroom was on the dated side but clean. He washed his hands, taking more time than usual to give his body a chance to settle down. On the way back to the kitchen, he passed the open door to what looked to be Chelsea's bedroom. He surveyed the room from the hall. A queen-size bed was on the far wall, with a night table and lamps on either side of the bed. On the other side of the room was a dresser with a bunch of bottles—perfume, hair products and who knew what else—on top. There were also framed photos. Several of her, Franklin and a woman who had to be Chelsea's mother based on the resemblance. One of her father, Chelsea and a woman Travis figured must be Chelsea's aunt. The second photo was of a younger man he didn't recognize. Maybe a boyfriend?

A knot of jealousy formed in his stomach.

"Everything okay in there?" Chelsea called out.

"On my way," he called back, leaving the doorway and striding back into the kitchen. "I'm ready to try this ragù."

Chelsea had set the table while he'd washed his hands. She plated the food and brought it to the table.

He took a bite, the flavors bursting in his mouth. "Wow," he said. "This is amazing."

Chelsea's eyes sparkled. "See, I told you. Better than spaghetti and meatballs, right?"

He agreed, and they ate in silence for a few moments, enjoying the meal. A part of him felt as if he should make conversation, but then he remembered this wasn't a date. And the silence wasn't bad. It was actually quite comfortable.

After a while, Chelsea cleared her throat. "Can I ask you a question?"

"Sure," he said hesitantly.

"Going to the state's attorney about the corruption in your department. That had to be hard."

That was an understatement. Two years after Brooks's

conviction, the FBI indicted several LAPD officers and detectives for bribery, money laundering and other crimes related to accepting money, gifts and other favors from local gang members to look the other way regarding their criminal activities. Not long after the initial news reports came out, Travis's name was leaked to the media as the source of the investigation that ultimately led to the charges. And then the organized campaign to ruin him kicked off. It had worked. Most of his colleagues wouldn't talk to him, refused to be partnered with him and certainly couldn't be trusted to have his back. He'd had no choice but to leave the force.

His stomach twisted. "That's not a question," he responded.

"I know. The question is why did you do it? I mean, you had to know you would be vilified even if the corrupt officers were arrested and charged."

He looked into her eyes. "I did it because it was the right thing to do."

She held his gaze for a long moment. She looked as if she was on the verge of a response, a response that he was surprisingly eager to hear, but the doorbell rang before she spoke.

"Excuse me," she said, getting up from the table and going to the door.

He waited until she disappeared from the kitchen to follow her. He heard the front door open, and then Chelsea spoke.

"Simon, what are you doing here?" she asked, irritation lacing her tone.

"One of my colleagues told me you were in the hospital last night. Why didn't you call me?"

Travis peeked around the corner, careful to stay out of

sight. Chelsea's back was to him, and the man—Simon, Chelsea had called him—hadn't noticed him. He took in the man's wavy black hair, blue eyes and beige-colored skin that shone in a way that could only be achieved with regular facials. He wore pressed chinos with a crease down the front and a starched white button-down. All he needed was a sweater thrown over his shoulders and the preppy look would be complete.

"Why would I call you?" Chelsea said.

The man sighed as if the answer was obvious, but Chelsea was just too dim-witted to see it. "Just because we aren't married anymore doesn't mean we can't care about each other, does it?"

"I haven't seen or heard from you in months, Simon. And when we were married, you cared so much about me that you cheated on me. Repeatedly."

Simon sighed again. "Chelsea, I want us to get past the past. We should look toward the future."

"We don't have a future."

"Can I please just come in? I don't want to have a conversation with you on the front porch for the whole neighborhood to hear."

Travis stepped around the wall separating the foyer from the rest of the house. "Chelsea, is everything okay here?"

Simon leaned around Chelsea. His eyes narrowed, and he made a show of sizing Travis up. "Who is this?"

"None of your business," Chelsea answered.

"This is my house," Simon shot back.

"Was your house. You seem to have forgotten I got the house in the divorce. You said it was a dump and you wanted to move to a condo on the beach."

Simon's expression turned contrite. "I said some things during our rough patch that I didn't mean. That's one of the things I wanted to talk to you about."

"I don't care what you want to talk about, Simon. I want you to leave." Chelsea started to close the door.

Simon's hand shot out, preventing it from closing. "Chelsea—" He stepped forward as if he was prepared to force his way into the house.

Travis crossed the few remaining steps separating him from Chelsea. He filled the space Simon would have used to slide past her into the house. "The lady asked you to leave," he said.

Simon was an inch or two shorter than Travis, but he looked up at him now with a glower. "I think you should leave. This conversation is between me and my wife."

"Ex-wife," Chelsea corrected. "Ex being the most important part, and if you don't leave now, I will call the cops."

"If you don't leave now, you will need an ambulance, not the police," Travis amended in a voice so cold it served as a warning.

Simon must have heard it. Anger still blazed in his gaze, but his hand dropped to his side, and he took several steps away from the door. His gaze swung to Chelsea, his expression turning pleading. "We need to talk, Chels. It's important. I'll call you to find a better time," he said.

"You do that." Chelsea closed the door. She turned to face Travis. "Sorry about that. I don't know what possessed him to show up here out of the blue. He's never done that before."

Travis held up his hands. "You don't owe me an explanation." And she didn't. Her ex-husband was clearly

an ass, but he had reminded Travis why he didn't do relationships. "I think we should take a look at those files
now," he said, turning his back on Chelsea, but not before
he saw something resembling hurt flash across her face.

Chapter Six

Chelsea cleared the kitchen table of their dinner plates and got a pot of coffee started while Travis moved into the dining room. The evening had taken on a decidedly chillier tone after Simon's unwelcome visit. She couldn't help but be annoyed at Travis's change in attitude after Simon left. She hadn't invited Simon over. But her ex-husband did have a way of rubbing people wrong. Unfortunately, she hadn't noticed that character flaw until after they'd said *I do.*

"Would you like some coffee?" Chelsea asked, heading for the kitchen ten steps away. Nothing in her small house was more than ten steps from anything else. Small was all she could afford, but she made the space feel like home.

"Yes. Black please," Travis answered.

She finished loading the dishes in the dishwasher and poured two cups of coffee. She brought the mugs to the table, setting his next to him, then carrying hers to sit across from him.

"You have done a lot of work in a short time." He flipped through the binder that held a timeline of Lily's last days.

"I've tried to reconstruct as much of the timeline as I could. It's been years, though, and there are still missing pieces." Chelsea reached across the cluttered table and pulled the second binder in front of her. She'd constructed biographies for each of the witnesses who testified in her father's case, including Lily's friends and family and the cops who had testified. She also had copies of relevant reports, news articles, internet posts and anything else that she could find relating to the case, but she could save those for later.

Her father had already told Travis about the last time he'd seen Lily. Now, she walked Travis through her father's trial and appeals, pulling documents from binders and boxes to support her statements as she went along. The recitation took hours, and by the time she was finished, she had covered the dining room table with papers.

She took a sip of the now-cold coffee, exhausted but also energized. She could see doubt about the case against her father in Travis's eyes. He'd taken copious notes and had asked a lot of questions, good questions, some of which she hadn't thought of.

He flipped through the binder to Lily's biography. "You've tried to contact Lily's friends and family?"

She nodded. "I was hoping someone might listen and at least concede that the police work wasn't as thorough as it could have been. Maybe support my dad's appeals, but none of Lily's family or friends would speak to me when I approached them about my father's possible innocence."

That wasn't completely true. A few of Lily's friends had plenty to say about what a monster her father was and how much they hoped he rotted in jail, but they wouldn't talk to her about anything that could help her prove his innocence. Even when she'd pointed out that if she was right and that her father was innocent, Lily's killer was still out there. She understood why Lily's friends and relatives didn't want to talk to the daughter of her accused murderer. She didn't blame them, but it made her investigation harder, and she couldn't help feeling some resentment toward them for it.

Travis flipped to the autopsy report. The description of Lily's wounds and the photos were gruesome. The brutal nature of the attack was one of the reasons the cops had been convinced the killer had to be someone who knew Lily and whose anger was personal.

"How did you get this?" Travis asked.

"If I told you, I'd have to kill you," she joked flatly.

The autopsy hadn't been easy to get. It had been part of the trial but wasn't included with the transcripts that were available to the public. She'd had to resort to searching the dark web for hackers and praying that she wasn't walking into a scam or a police sting. It had not been cheap, but it had worked. The hacker had gotten her the autopsy report and the police report in the case. She paid and hadn't asked any questions.

Travis's eyebrows rose.

"It's better you don't know. Let's just say with enough money, anything is attainable."

He seemed to let it go. For now. "How long have you been trying to free your father?" Travis asked.

She met his gaze straight on. "Since the day he was arrested."

Travis's brow rose. "You believe that much in his innocence?"

"Yes," she said, steel in her voice. "He is innocent." She'd never believed in anything more than that her father, for all his faults, would never kill anyone. "My father loved Lily. And she loved him. I think that's why she met him that night at the bar. She may not have wanted to be with him, but she still cared about him. He didn't do this." It didn't escape her notice that her statement echoed Simon's comments from earlier. "And I won't stop until I prove he's innocent."

"Okay," Travis said with a nod.

Her shoulders relaxed when she saw that even if Travis didn't quite believe in her father's innocence yet, he at least believed that she believed it. That was a start. At least she wasn't completely alone in this anymore. Her father now had one person on his side with the knowledge, expertise and resources that could lead to his freedom.

Travis flipped several pages in the binder. "We need to speak with Peter Schmeichel and Gina McGrath. If Peter admits that he lied and Gina confirms it, that could go a long way to getting a judge's attention."

"Gina used to live next door to Lily. She worked as a nurse. I went to the house after I got the note about Peter's confession, but Gina doesn't live there anymore. The current occupant has been living there for years and had never heard of Gina." Chelsea grabbed the photos she'd taken of Lily's old house. She'd taken them more than a decade after the murder, but the home hadn't changed much in those years. "In the statement Gina gave the police on the night of Lily's murder, she says she was taking the trash out and saw my dad and Lily arguing on the porch. That was hours before the medical examiner says Lily was killed. My dad admits to the argument, but he swears he left and Lily was alive."

"Gina didn't see him leave?" Travis's eyes darted over the testimony.

"No. She went back into her house before my dad left."

Travis gave the note accusing Peter of lying a quick

once-over, then flipped through the file until he got to the section on Peter. "And what can you tell me about Peter?"

"He was Gina's boyfriend back then," Chelsea admitted. "According to Peter's testimony, he left Gina's place the night of the murder around 1:00 a.m. He says he saw my dad leaving Lily's house at the same time. That my dad was disheveled and in a rush. His statement is what put my father at Lily's house around the time the medical examiner says she was killed." She flipped to a different page in the binder. "Mr. Schmeichel has a criminal record for dealing drugs, assault and burglary. Amazingly, he's managed not to do all that much time in prison even though he's a career criminal. He was arrested a week after Lily's death and that's when he told the cops about seeing my dad at Lily's house."

"And you find that suspicious," Travis stated the obvious.

"Of course I do. Why wouldn't he have approached the cops earlier if he'd really seen my dad that night?" She turned to yet another page in her binder. "And Gina's statement says Peter was at her house all night. No mention of him leaving at 1:00 a.m."

Travis frowned. "Could be an oversight. Witness statements often don't match exactly."

"The cops didn't interview Peter right after the murder. At least, there's not a statement from him that I could find."

"We need to talk to him," Travis conceded.

"His last known address is in the binder, but he's not exactly what I'd call stable. I can't say for sure that he still lives there."

"We'll find him wherever he is," Travis said with confidence. He looked up from the notebook, the gaze he pinned on her intense. "You've done a good job with this so far. Better than some professional private investigators I've had the misfortune to run into."

She nodded her thanks for the compliment and lowered her gaze to the papers on the table. Her cheeks were on fire, and her heart was thundering. "You guys should consider hiring more teachers. There's no one more resourceful on the planet."

Travis grinned and her stomach did a flip-flop. "I'll keep that in mind," he said.

CHELSEA WAS DAMN IMPRESSIVE. When Travis thought about what life must have been like for her since her father went to prison, he felt for her. "Tell me about Lily," he said.

Chelsea moved to open the binder to Lily's page.

Travis put his hand over hers, stopping her from flipping the pages. "You knew her. Tell me about her in your own words."

He could see genuine grief on her face when she thought about Lily. "What do you want to know?"

"Tell me how she and your father met. What was their relationship like? What did you think about her?"

"I was nineteen when they met. Between work and school, I was busy and not around very much, but she was nice. I was glad my dad had someone who seemed to care about him. He and my mother had married young, and then they had me. My mother passed away when I was ten, and my father dated a lot while I was growing up, but Lily was his first serious girlfriend after my mom passed. She did my hair for me for free, and we both loved action movies, so we'd always catch opening weekend of the new ones together. She was just great. She treated me more like a little sister than her boyfriend's daughter."

It was clear Lily's father hadn't been the only one who'd loved Lily. "How did you feel about her breaking up with your dad?"

Chelsea's gaze slid away from his. "I didn't really have an opinion."

Travis waited a beat, but Chelsea didn't add any more. "If this is going to work, you have to be honest with me. About everything."

"I'm not lying." But Chelsea still wasn't meeting his gaze.

"Maybe not, but you're holding back."

Chelsea sighed. "You already know my dad was a heavy drinker back then. He was never violent, but he could be really mean when he had too many. I suspect Lily got tired of it."

She flipped to the page with Lily's biography. Hers was one of the only profiles that had a photo with it. Lily had been quite beautiful with a slim, heart-shaped face and straight dark hair. Her dark brown eyes were ringed with gold on the outer edges, and laugh lines creased the edges of her mouth.

Chelsea rubbed her thumb over the photograph as if she could touch Lily's cheek. Her gaze shifted out the window. It was clear that she'd been transported back into her memories. Travis wanted to reach across the table and comfort her. He suspected that she needed it. With her aunt not believing in her father's innocence and her father in prison, she was isolated. Alone.

And he needed to remember that. She was vulnerable, and she'd come to him for help.

"I skimmed Lily's half sister's testimony at the trial," Travis said. "She said Lily was finished with your father. That it was over, and she made that clear to him.

Lily was dating someone else. But she didn't say who that person was."

"We never found out who the other man was. If there was another man. If Lily was seeing someone new, why did she meet my dad at the bar that night? And it seems odd that Lily told no one about him."

"Your dad also said Lily told him she was seeing someone new."

Chelsea shrugged. "Maybe that was her way of letting him down easy. I don't know. But I know that Lily's family, the cops, the prosecutors, everyone decided my father had committed the murder just hours after Lily's body was found. They never looked at anyone else seriously."

They were going to have to find a way to get Lily's friends and family to talk to them if they wanted to find out if her mystery man existed. He didn't anticipate that it was going to be easy.

Chelsea looked deflated, and he didn't like it. He preferred the aggressive, take-charge, uber-organized woman on a mission to save her father. He wasn't sure he believed her father was innocent, but he admired her determination. And he wanted to give her closure. One way or the other. He had a feeling that it had been some time since she had genuinely smiled. For one fleeting moment, the urge to be the man who put that smile on her face consumed him.

"Do you know the name of the salon where Lily worked?" he asked instead.

"The salon she worked at closed a few years ago. But I know Lily's best friend and former coworker, Rachel Lamier, opened her own salon, Snips, in Venice. She wouldn't talk to me when I called her, though."

"We have to start somewhere. Maybe I'll have better

luck. If you're up for it, we can pay a visit to Rachel to-morrow morning."

"I'm up for it, definitely."

"Great." Travis looked at his watch. "It's getting late so I think I should go." He rose.

She stood and walked him to the door.

"Make sure you lock this behind me." He tapped the lock.

"Don't worry about me."

But he was worried about her. He'd made a promise to her father to watch out for her, and he intended to keep that promise. "Good night, Chelsea. Sleep tight."

Chapter Seven

Chelsea spent a restless night flitting in and out of sleep. A part of her was excited. She felt like there was finally some movement behind her investigation. Another part of her was nervous. This was her father's last chance. If she didn't find some evidence to convince the authorities that they'd convicted the wrong man for Lily's murder, her father would spend the rest of his life in jail.

At 7:00 a.m., she gave up trying to sleep and went to the basement where she kept her treadmill. A forty-five-minute workout burned off some of her nervousness, but her injured hip throbbed afterward. She took a long hot shower to soothe the pain and, when she got out, found a text message from Travis telling her he was on his way over. She dressed quickly in a yellow floral dress and braided her long light brown hair into a goddess braid encircling her head. She was still debating which pair of sandals went best with the outfit when the doorbell rang.

Travis stood on her doorstep, two steaming to-go cups in hand. Despite the already warm late June morning, he wore blue jeans. He'd paired them with a white short-sleeved collared shirt that brought out the flecks of gray in his brown eyes. Not for the first time, she noted how devastatingly handsome the man was.

Travis's brow quirked up. "Can I come in?"

Chelsea's body flooded with embarrassment at how long she'd been standing in the doorway thinking about him. "Yes. Of course. Sorry."

She stepped back to allow him to pass by her into the house. He headed straight for the dining room, where she had cleared a small square of space on the table for her laptop. She'd spent some time after he left the night before scouring social media for more of Lily's prior co-workers with no luck.

"How was your night?" she asked, accepting the cup of coffee Travis handed her. "Thank you." She popped the lid off her coffee and took a sip. She was pleasantly surprised to find it was exactly how she liked it, with milk and more sugar than she probably should have had. She was touched that he had paid attention to the several cups of coffee she'd plowed through while they'd worked the day before. She closed her eyes and wrapped her hands around the warm cup, taking another sip. It was good. Almost as good as the expensive stuff she bought from the specialty coffee shop not far from her house, her one splurge.

She opened her eyes and found Travis watching her, his gaze intense. Sexual awareness flooded through her. "What?"

"Nothing." He shifted his gaze away, focusing on setting up his tablet next to her laptop. "How are you feeling? Any pain?"

Part of her wanted to push to know exactly what he was thinking when he was looking at her, but she let it go. "A little. Nothing a couple of ibuprofen can't fix. Did you have any luck finding our eyewitness Peter Schmeichel?"

"I think I have a line on him."

"Really?" She felt herself perking up at the news. "That's great."

"Don't get too excited. I don't have anything concrete like a location yet, but I'm working on it."

"Still, great." She took another sip of her coffee. "Hopefully, Rachel will give us some useful information as well. Snips opens at nine."

Travis looked at his wristwatch. "It's still early. The shop won't be open yet."

Chelsea put her coffee down and eyed her phone. "Are you sure it wouldn't be better for me to call and make an appointment when they open? Rachel might be more receptive to answering our questions if we don't ambush her."

Travis shook his hand. "I come from the school of thought where it's better to ask forgiveness than permission."

"Alrighty then. An ambush it is," Chelsea teased. "I'm just going to go finish getting dressed."

In the bathroom, she popped open the bottle of ibuprofen and took two pills, then brushed her teeth and reapplied her lip gloss before rejoining Travis.

"What are you doing now?" She looked over his shoulder at the screen of his tablet.

"Just pulling on some of the threads, one of which I hope will lead to Peter Schmeichel. He's done a good job of staying under the radar. He hasn't filed taxes in years or applied for disability or unemployment. I can't find any relatives or even an address for him."

Chelsea frowned. "I thought you said you had a line on him."

"I have other oars in the water, don't worry," he responded confidently. "I'll find him. It's just unusual for someone to disappear so completely."

"Do you think there's something to it? Like maybe he's disappeared to avoid someone or something. Like the law?"

Travis shrugged. "Maybe. I'll keep digging."

Since they had an hour to kill before they needed to leave for Snips, Travis continued his search for Peter while she tried to locate as many of Lily's former coworkers as she could. It was slow going; most salons didn't list their stylists by name, so she had to cobble together information from old websites and social media. Travis didn't seem to be having much better luck based on his grunts and sighs.

At ten minutes to 9:00 a.m., Travis closed the cover of his tablet. "Are you ready to head out to see Rachel?"

Chelsea closed her laptop. "As ready as I'll ever be."

They climbed into Travis's car, and he headed for Venice. Rachel had opened her shop, Snips, six years earlier. Based on its fashionable location, it seemed like she was doing very well as a business owner. Rachel had been interviewed by the police during their investigation, but she hadn't testified at Chelsea's father's trial. Chelsea didn't know what or if Rachel could tell them anything that might be helpful in proving her father's innocence, but she hoped the woman would be less hostile toward now that more time had passed. She was still hopeful Rachel might be able to tell them something about Lily's life around the time of her murder that they didn't already know. Maybe point them in the direction of this mysterious boyfriend, assuming he existed at all.

They parked in a garage and walked the two blocks to the salon. Chelsea noticed several women turn and shoot very feminine gazes and smiles at Travis as they made the trek to the salon. A pang of jealousy stirred inside her, but Travis didn't seem to notice the women's stares. Or maybe he was just used to them. He was a very attractive man, there was no doubt about that. Maybe if they'd met under different circumstances... But they hadn't. And she needed to focus all her attention on her father's case.

One of the women passing by them tripped on some uneven pavement she hadn't noticed because she'd been staring at Travis.

He reached out a hand, steadying her. "Are you okay?"

"Yeah...yes. Thank you." The woman's words came out breathily.

Chelsea rolled her eyes and shot a death glare at the woman. The woman's cheeks pinked, and she hurried on.

Travis turned to her, his eyes sparkling with mischief. "That wasn't very nice."

"She's a grown woman falling all over herself because you have a nice—"

He looked like he was trying not to laugh. "A nice what?"

"I'm sure you know you're a very attractive man."

"Am I now?" Travis said in a teasing tone.

"Can we just get to the salon, please?" Chelsea picked up her pace.

Now Travis did let loose with a hearty laugh. "Slow down. I want to hear more about how attractive you find me."

"I did not say I found you attractive," she shot back, heat flooding into her cheeks. "I said you know you are an attractive man."

"A very attractive man, you said."

"Is this really the time for this conversation?" she asked, nearly sweating with embarrassment.

Travis caught her arm as they arrived in front of Snips. "I think it's a great time for this conversation."

A gust of wind blew a napkin down the street, but it did nothing to cool the heat burning through her.

Travis stared at her with an odd look she couldn't place on his face. "I think you're very attractive, too."

Chelsea's heart thumped in her chest, her pulse picking up even more steam when Travis took a step closer to her. She could see that his brown eyes were rimmed in gold. She saw heat in them.

Travis reached out a hand, running two fingers down her cheek, sending her into a full-body blush. He leaned in closer, and she closed her eyes.

Someone bumped into her shoulder. Chelsea glanced at the woman and recognized her as Rachel from her social media accounts.

Rachel Lamier had shiny, bouncy, shoulder-length red hair that only a professional could have achieved. It framed her square-shaped face and deep-set blue eyes. Rachel appeared to be about the same age as Lily would have been. Chelsea couldn't help but feel a twinge of sadness at the thought that Lily hadn't had the opportunity to live the years that Rachel had.

Rachel tore her gaze from Travis, who was seemingly the cause of their minor collision, and turned to Chelsea. "Oh, sorry. I wasn't looking where I was going."

Chelsea chuckled knowingly. "That's okay. I understand. You are Rachel, aren't you?"

The slightly amused expression on Rachel's face changed to suspicion. "Yes. Do I know you?"

"I'm Chelsea Harper. I'm actually here to speak with you."

Rachel's shoulders relaxed. "Oh, well, I have a client scheduled in a few minutes but if you can come back this afternoon, I'm free after 1:00 p.m." Rachel shot another glance at Travis, no doubt wondering about his presence.

"I'm not here to have my hair done. I was hoping to speak to you about Lily Wong."

Rachel started. "Lily? Why?"

It was Chelsea's turn to shoot a glance at Travis. He picked up on her train of thought right away. "Ms. Harper is Franklin Brooks's daughter." Travis handed Rachel a business card. "She has hired me to look into her father's case."

"I don't have anything to say to you," Rachel spat.

"My father is innocent," Chelsea replied firmly.

"We'll only take a moment of your time," Travis interjected. "Please."

The seconds stretched until Chelsea was sure Rachel was going to say no and walk away. But Rachel surprised her. "Ten minutes. Then I have to prepare for my client. What do you want to know about Lily?"

RACHEL LED CHELSEA and Travis to her office at the back of the salon and closed the door. The office was no bigger than a closet and so cluttered as to be claustrophobic. Rachel cleared off the sole chair in front of her desk, and Travis gestured for Chelsea to take it. She did, and he stood next to her facing Rachel who took a seat behind the desk.

"I don't know how I can help you," Rachel said. "It's been a long time, and the cops caught Lily's murderer as far as I'm concerned." She shot a venomous look in Chelsea's direction.

Even though he understood where Rachel was coming from, Travis felt a surge of protectiveness. Chelsea didn't deserve anger from Lily's friends and family. Even if her father was a murderer, she'd done nothing wrong. And if she was right, and Franklin was innocent, she was one of the bravest women he knew.

Chelsea didn't seem to be letting Rachel get to her, though. Her expression remained polite, almost as if she hadn't seen the nasty look Rachel shot at her, although Travis knew that she had.

"We understand why you feel that way," Travis said soothingly. "You want someone to pay for what was done to your friend."

"I do, yes."

"But what if the wrong person is in jail? What if Lily's killer is still out there? Walking free? You wouldn't want an innocent man to pay for a crime he didn't commit."

Rachel bit her bottom lip. "Of course I wouldn't want that."

"Me, either. That's why I agreed to take this case. If Lily's killer is still out there, we need to find him and have him brought to justice. Anything you can tell us, no matter how insignificant you might think it is, could help."

From the look on her face, his words had gotten through to Rachel. "I'll tell you what I can, but I warn you it probably won't be much."

"Thank you." Travis smiled, melting more of Rachel's iciness. "Can you tell me what Lily was like?"

Rachel smiled. "She was the most caring person you'd ever meet. Everyone from her coworkers to her clients loved her." It was similar to the way Franklin and Chelsea had described Lily. Of course, people tended to speak well of the dead even when they hadn't been very nice people in life, but he had a feeling that Lily had genuinely been a good person who was liked by many.

"Did you and Lily hang out a lot outside of work?" he asked.

"I wouldn't say a lot, but we did hang out a few times."

It looked like Chelsea had wisely decided to let him take the lead on questioning Rachel, so he forged on. "Did Lily ever mention a new boyfriend?"

Rachel's face scrounged as if she was thinking back. "No, not that I remember. She broke up with Frank a few weeks before she was killed." She shot another look Chelsea's way, but this one was far less venomous. "I don't remember her talking about dating anyone new."

"Did she ever talk about Frank with you? Do you know why they broke up?"

Rachel nodded. "Yes, she talked about him all the time. She really loved him, but I got the feeling that she was fed up with his drinking near the end. I don't think she wanted to end it, but she didn't know what else to do. Or how to help him. She stopped hanging out with me as much after work once they broke up. I don't know much about the relationship after that."

Travis poked and prodded along that line of questioning for a bit more, but Rachel didn't have more to offer about Lily and Frank's relationship.

"Is there anything else you can remember about that time?"

"Well, there was one thing. Lily had been having some trouble at her house."

Chelsea sat up straighter in the chair next to him. "What kind of trouble?"

"She complained a couple of times about some strange stuff that was happening. Her car had been vandalized with someone throwing eggs on her hood. And she thought someone had been in her house, but nothing was missing. I told her it was probably just teenagers goofing, you know. It didn't seem serious."

"Did she call the police?"

"I don't think so. Like I said, we both thought it was probably just some of the rowdy teens who lived in her neighborhood. And it wasn't like there was anything missing or permanently damaged." Rachel shrugged. "What were the police going to do?"

Probably nothing, but he made a mental note to check if Lily had filed a police report anyway. "Did you tell the police about the vandalism when they interviewed you?"

"Oh." Rachel seemed surprised by the question. "I'm not sure. Probably not. They seemed so sure that Frank had done it when they talked to me. Most of their questions were about him, and his and Lily's relationship."

Travis shot a look at Chelsea. She was pressing her lips together as if she was trying not to let certain words spill out of her mouth.

Rachel pressed a hand over her mouth. "You don't think the stuff with her house had anything to do with her murder, do you? I mean…" She cut a look at Chelsea. "If Frank is innocent, and I didn't say anything…"

"Right now, we are collecting information. We don't know what is relevant and what isn't, but you've been very helpful." Travis rose as did Chelsea next to him. "If you think of anything else, give me a call."

He opened the door, but Rachel spoke again before he and Chelsea stepped out of the office. "I met Frank a couple of times. When a cop said he killed Lily, I couldn't see it. I know people have dark sides, but he just didn't seem like the type. He loved her. You could see that whenever they were together. Even when they were fighting and arguing."

Chelsea gave a small smile. "Thank you for saying that."

Rachel tapped the side of Travis's business card against the palm of her hand. "Would you let me know what happens? If it wasn't Frank who killed Lily, I'd like to know. I want to see the person who hurt my friend in jail."

"I will." Chelsea nodded. "And like Travis said, if you can think of anything else, please let him know."

They headed out of the salon. Travis glanced at Chelsea as they walked to the car in silence, but she looked lost in her thoughts. He'd give anything to know what she was thinking, but her face gave away nothing. They were back in the car before she spoke again.

"Well, what do you think?" she asked, fastening her seat belt.

"The vandalism and possible break-in are something to explore. I take it you didn't know about that." Travis started the car and pulled out of the parking lot.

"I didn't. And if my dad did, he never said anything to me. And it didn't come up during his trial either," Chelsea added bitterly.

He could understand why she might be bitter. It certainly would have helped her father if the jury had heard that Lily had been the victim of vandalism and possible break-ins just weeks before she was murdered. Of course, it might have also hurt him if the prosecution had been able to imply that Franklin was behind the vandalism and break-in. You never knew with a jury.

"Rachel wasn't sure if Lily called the police, but I'm going to check into whether she made a police report about the events at her house," he said, laying out his next steps.

"Okay, and what should I do?"

"Did Lily have any social media presence?"

Chelsea nodded. "Yes, she had a couple social media pages. Why?"

"Take another look at them. We need to figure out if this boyfriend really existed. If he did, it's likely he's in those feeds somewhere. Don't just look for the obvious, though. Look for anything out of the ordinary for Lily. A new restaurant. Changes to her normal routine. Anything that might have changed between the time she and your father broke up until her death."

Chelsea frowned. "Rachel didn't seem to think Lily had a new man in her life."

"That's what she said, but I noticed some hesitation. Like maybe there was something she didn't want to say. Often people don't want to say anything that might make their friends look bad, especially when those friends can no longer defend themselves."

Chelsea shrugged. "Okay, I'll see what I can find."

"In the meantime, are you up for a little field trip?"

"A field trip? Where?"

"I want to get a look at Lily's old house. Get a feel for the place and the neighborhood and how someone might have gotten in and out without being seen."

The air in the car stilled. Lily's old house...which also happened to be the scene of her murder.

"I understand if you don't want to go with me. I can drop you off at your place if you want."

"No," Chelsea said quickly. "No, I'll go with you."

"Chelsea, you really don't have to—"

"It's okay. It's been a long time, and I want to be involved in every part of the investigation."

"Okay. Let's go back to the beginning." Travis said, turning the car in the direction of Lily's old San Fernando Valley neighborhood.

Chapter Eight

Chelsea gave Travis an address that she knew by heart, and he plugged it into the GPS and drove. He stopped the car across the street from Lily's old house. It looked bigger, cheerier the last time she'd seen it. Lily had been proud of her little home, keeping the square patch of front lawn neat and trimmed and the window boxes full of flowers and herbs. Now it looked as if the current owners hadn't put any effort into its upkeep.

Travis turned to her. "You can stay in the car. I just want to take a quick look around."

Her gaze didn't leave the forlorn little house, but she answered him. "No, I want to go with you."

They climbed out of the car together. Chelsea stopped at the top of the cracked walkway and looked at the house. The house itself hadn't changed, but it had lost its sheen. Gone were the colorful flowers in the flower beds. The lawn was overgrown. The windows were filthy with grime and dirt.

Chelsea pointed to the house to the right of Lily's old place. "That's where Gina McGrath lived."

The neighboring house looked only slightly better kept than Lily's. Chelsea knew from her investigation that Gina no longer lived there.

She and Travis made their way up the cracked walkway to the front door. Travis knocked on the door, then peered through the front window. "I don't think anyone is living here at the moment."

Somehow that made her even sadder. Lily was gone, and her house was empty.

"I'm going to head around back," Travis said. "See if I can find an open door and take a look around."

Chelsea nodded. "Let's go."

Travis hesitated for a moment, searching her face. Whatever he found there clearly didn't please him, but it must have been enough to let him know she wasn't going to fall apart on him.

They walked through the tall grass around to the back of the house. Although the back door was locked, it was flimsy enough that Travis needed only to give it a good shove to get it to pop open.

"Travis," Chelsea hissed. "That's illegal."

"I'm just going to take a look. Get a feel for the crime scene. You can stay here if you want."

They both knew she wasn't going to do that despite her protests.

She hadn't been in Lily's house since before the murder and then only a handful of times. There was a generously spacious living room/kitchen/dining room setup followed by a short hall. Travis was right. There was clearly no one currently living in the house. There was no food in the fridge, and the water and electricity had been shut off. The sun was still high in the sky, but with no lights to turn on inside the house, shadows crisscrossed the space.

Travis aimed the flashlight on his phone toward the hall. Chelsea followed him past a bathroom and a small bedroom. Lily's bedroom was at the end of the hall. A king-size bed still rested against one wall, its headboard leaning precariously forward.

Chelsea's mind flashed back to the crime-scene pictures from the file her hacker had gotten for her. Lily lying on the bed. Cuts on her face, neck and hands. Her sheets were covered with blood. The report indicated she had fought. Her nails had been broken off in several places. And she had been stabbed six times. *Overkill*, Chelsea remembered reading in the detective's notes. It was one of the reasons the police believed Lily had more than likely known her attacker.

Chelsea was suddenly overwhelmed by a wave of emotion. The room was too small, and everything in it was too close to her. She'd looked at the crime-scene photos dozens of times, but somehow, she'd been able to detach in a way she couldn't while standing in Lily's old room. In the space where she'd been killed.

Almost as if he could feel her inner turmoil, Travis reached out and pulled her into his arms.

"Breathe. Just breathe slowly."

"All the violence, the anger. He stabbed her six times. Why?" Tears slid from her eyes.

Travis laid his cheek on her head, pulling her in closer. "I don't know, honey. I do know whoever did this is a coward. And we are going to figure it out."

She leaned into his warmth, letting the spicy scent of his cologne wrap around her. Despite the circumstances, in that moment, she felt safe. Protected. She stepped out of his arms, wiping the tears from her cheeks. "Can we get out of here?"

They retraced their steps through the house to the back door. They rounded the house just as a man got out of a red Mazda in the driveway next door.

He looked at them, surprise on his face. "Hello? Can I help you?" A curly mop of brunette curls bounced on the man's head as he pulled himself the rest of the way out of his car and slammed the driver's-side door.

Travis made his way forward, his business card extended toward the man. "I'm Travis Collins, a private investigator. This is Chelsea Harper, my associate. We're looking into the death of the woman who used to live here."

"Lily," the man said.

Chelsea shared a quick look with Travis.

"Yes," Travis confirmed. "Did you know her?"

"A little," the man answered. He looked to be a few years younger than her father, mid- to late-forties.

"Would you mind if I asked your name?"

"I'm Jace Orson."

"And how long have you lived here, Mr. Orson?"

Jace darted a glance at his house as if he was thinking about making a run for it. "About eight years. A little closer to nine."

"So, you lived here when Lily lived next door," Chelsea said.

"Yes. It was so sad when she was... Well, you obviously know if you're investigating. I thought they caught the guy who did it. A boyfriend or something."

"There have been some new developments," Travis said quickly.

Jace's face registered surprise.

Chelsea frowned. She had a feeling he'd spoken up so quickly to cut off her chance to argue that the man in jail for Lily's death had been wrongly convicted.

"Do you remember seeing anything unusual around the time that Lily was killed?" Travis asked. "Maybe a stranger hanging around? Or a vehicle that seemed out of place?"

"No." Jace shook his head. "But it's been a long time. I would have told the police if I had."

"Do you remember seeing or hearing Lily argue with anyone? Ever see her upset with anyone?"

"Well, sometimes she and the boyfriend of hers got into it." He rolled his eyes. "Loudly. I don't know what she saw in him. I could tell he was a loser. I wish she had listened to me."

Chelsea stopped angry words from springing forward and instead asked, "Listened to you?"

"Yeah, I may have mentioned that she could do better than the bum she was seeing. For a while there, I actually thought she had taken my advice."

"Why?" Travis asked.

"Because a new guy started coming around for a while, but he wasn't around for long before the loser boyfriend was back."

Chelsea's heart pounded. "The new guy, do you remember his name?"

"No, sorry. I don't think I ever knew it. Like I said, I didn't know Lily that well."

Well enough to call her boyfriend a loser, Chelsea thought, still fuming.

"Can you describe the man you saw?" Travis pressed.

"Oh, man. No, I don't think so. I'm only even thinking about this stuff because you guys asked. I try not to remember what happened right next door to me."

"I understand," Travis said in a conciliatory tone. "Do you happen to remember where you were when Lily was killed?"

Jace frowned. "I don't think I like what you are suggesting."

"Trust me I'm not suggesting anything," Travis said with a smile. "I'm just trying to draw as complete a picture as possible of the last moments of Lily's life."

Jace hesitated for a moment before answering. "Well, I do remember where I was as it happens. I was out with friends that night."

"One more question for you. Do you know where the neighbor on the other side of Lily's house moved to?"

Jace looked over Chelsea's shoulder at the house that used to be Gina's. "Sorry. She hung around for a little while after Lily died, but a lot of people got freaked out by a murder happening on their street. And, well, a lot has changed over the years."

"Thanks anyway for your help," Travis said, grabbing Chelsea's hand and backing away. "If you think of anything else, could you please give me a call at the number on the card? Anything you remember could be helpful."

"He's not going to call," Chelsea said as they got back into the car. She watched Jace watch them for a moment before he went into his house and shut the door.

"That's okay. He confirmed that another man had been visiting Lily around the time of her death. We need to find that man."

Chapter Nine

"Where to next?" Chelsea asked when they were back in the car.

"I'm headed back to my office to see if I can track down Peter and Gina. I'm taking you home so you can get some rest."

"I don't need to rest." But something about saying the word set off a yawn.

"You do need to rest. You could have been killed, and I noticed that hitch in your step back at Lily's house. Your hip is hurting you."

"I'll be fine."

"Rest. Investigations take time. A lot of the work is waiting for something to break."

Frustration swelled in her chest. "My father has been in jail for seven years now. I don't want to waste any more time."

Travis glanced across the car at her. "I get it, I do. I'll call you if I get any news. Until then, there's nothing for you to do."

She didn't like it, but she wasn't willing to argue with him about it. Not when she had an idea about who might be able to help them. But she knew Travis would want to go with her, and in this case, she was sure she needed to make this visit alone.

He turned into her driveway moments later. Travis walked her to her door and waited on the porch until he heard the lock click into place. She watched as he backed out of her driveway and waited five minutes before she grabbed her purse and keys and headed back out.

She'd made the short drive from her place to her father's best friend's house hundreds of times over the years. Bill Rowland, or Uncle Bill as she'd called him since she was a little girl, was a second father to her...

She turned the radio to her favorite nineties pop station and willed the tension in her shoulders to let up.

A short time later, she pulled to a stop at the curb in front of a suburban brick ranch in Winnetka. The flower beds lining the front of the house were filled with neatly trimmed flowers and hedges, and the grass was freshly cut. A tall maple tree stood stoically in the yard, his green leaves waving in the slight breeze cooling the day. Uncle Bill had taken up gardening in his semiretirement with the same passion he'd had for his auto mechanic business.

She walked to the front door and rang the bell. Seconds later, the door swung open, and Uncle Bill stood before her.

Uncle Bill smiled, happy to see her as always. The joy on his face sent a pang of guilt through her for not visiting more often. Uncle Bill had never married or had children. He had a brother in Arizona, but for the most part he'd always been on his own. Chelsea and her father were his family. He had been there for her as much as Aunt Brenda had, even though the two hadn't always seen eye to eye. Brenda Harper was conservative, quiet, a rule follower at heart. And Uncle Bill...was not. Gregarious, outgoing, always up for a laugh, that was Uncle Bill. He'd kept the same boisterous personality into his retirement years.

"How's life treating you, kid?" he asked, grabbing her into a bear hug. He held her there for a moment before pulling back and searching her face. "Everything good?"

Uncle Bill was one of the most empathetic people she knew. Which was why he'd always known when she was feeling down or nervous or needed someone to talk to.

Chelsea nodded and forced a smile. "Yes, everything is fine."

"Are you teaching this summer?" he asked as he led her into the small living room where a glass of lemonade and a small plate of cookies rested on the coffee table in front of his lounger.

"Not this summer. I decided to take some time off."

"Good for you. Oh, let me get you a glass of lemonade. I got chocolate chip cookies from this new bakery near the grocery store. They aren't too bad," he said, turning for the kitchen.

"No, Uncle Bill, I'm not thirsty or hungry. I just need to talk to you."

He turned back to her. "Are you sure?"

She assured him that she didn't want any refreshments, and he reclaimed his glass of already poured lemonade before settling into his battered brown easy chair.

Despite an active lifestyle, he'd begun to develop a little pouch in his tummy. At fifty-four years old, Uncle Bill was fortunate to have worked hard, built a sound business and saved enough that he only went into work a couple of days a week now. The rest of the workweek he left to his shop manager and employees, most of whom had worked for him for years, to handle. Her father had been one of those employees before he was arrested and convicted of Lily's murder. Uncle Bill had never believed his best friend was a murderer and had even offered to pay to hire a better lawyer for her father. But Franklin's pride hadn't allowed him to accept what he considered charity. Not even from his best friend.

"So, what brings you to an old man's door today?"

"You are not an old man, and I'm sorry I don't visit more often."

Uncle Bill waved her comment away. "Ah, don't worry about it. You're young. You have a life to live. I get it. So, what brings you by today?" he repeated.

Chelsea sat on the edge of her uncle's brown leather sofa, considering how to ease into the conversation she needed to have. Deciding that there was no easy way to ask, she just plunged in. "I need to ask you something, and it might be a little upsetting."

Uncle Bill frowned. He placed his lemonade on the coffee table. "You're scaring me. Are you sick?"

"No, no, it's nothing like that."

"Is it your aunt?" Aunt Brenda and Uncle Bill didn't get along, but Chelsea knew he would do anything for her aunt because of her.

"No, she's fine, too. We're both fine." Chelsea took a deep breath. "I've hired a private investigator to help me prove Dad didn't kill Lily."

Uncle Bill looked at her, his face twisted with surprise. It took him a moment to speak. "What? Why?"

"Why? Because he's innocent. And I need your help proving it."

"Chelsea—"

"Could you just answer some of my questions, please?" she interjected before he could argue with her.

Uncle Bill sighed. "Sure, you know I'll tell you whatever you want to know."

"Well, during my investigation, I found out a couple

of things that I didn't know about Dad and Lily's relationship."

"Things like what?"

"Did Dad ever tell you that Lily was seeing someone else?"

Uncle Bill looked uncomfortable. "I don't know if I should be talking to you about your father and Lily's relationship."

"Uncle Bill, I'm not a child. This could be important."

"At the end there, when your dad and Lily were finally calling it quits, he might've suspected she was seeing someone else. But I don't think he had any real proof."

"I spoke to Dad. He said Lily told him she was seeing someone else."

Uncle Bill's eyes went wide, and he pushed himself up straighter in his chair. "Yes…yes, but your father said she wouldn't tell him who the other man was."

"That's right. She didn't tell anyone his name, and the prosecution wasn't able to figure out who he was."

Her uncle slumped back down in his chair. "Honey, you know how emotional breakups can be."

That she did. Her recent confrontation with Simon flashed through her head before she shook it away. This wasn't about her and Simon. It was about her father and Lily.

The police never even considered this new guy, but if Lily had been seeing him, the man could know something about her murder. Or be her murderer. "I know you were only friends with Lily through Dad, but did you suspect she was seeing someone? Do you have any idea who this person might be?"

Uncle Bill's gaze slid away from hers. "I don't know, honey. It was all a very long time ago."

It felt as if he was holding something back, but she didn't know how to get him to tell her what it was. Just like her father, Uncle Bill's first concern was always protecting her even when she didn't need protecting.

"Why are you digging into this now?" he asked. "I thought your father's conviction had been upheld on appeal?"

"It was. The only chance he has now is to prove his innocence. And that's what I'm going to do."

Uncle Bill sighed. "I'm sure your father wouldn't want you to spend your time like this."

"Like what?" She threw her hands up in frustration. "Getting an innocent man out of jail? I can't think of a better way to spend my time."

Uncle Bill scooted to the end of his chair and reached out to take her hands. "I'm just worried that this obsession isn't healthy for you."

"Uncle Bill, an injustice has been done." She knew she sounded like a zealot. Maybe she was, but was zealotry in the interest of justice so wrong?

Uncle Bill dropped her hands and looked away.

"What is it?" she asked.

He held his gaze on the picture window for a long moment before turning back to her. "Chelsea, your father has exhausted his appeals. Every court that has looked at his case has determined he is guilty."

"What are you saying?"

His sigh this time was heavier and laced with something she couldn't quite name. Regret, maybe. "Maybe we have to face a hard truth."

"A hard truth? You mean that my father killed Lily? It sounds like you have already faced this truth."

"I've offered to hire better attorneys for your father, several times. He's always refused."

"He's proud."

"Or he feels guilty. Maybe he feels like he deserves the punishment he's getting."

"He has always professed his innocence. And he has appealed his conviction."

Uncle Bill shook his head. "He pursued that appeal for you. Because you wanted him to."

A heavy silence fell over the room while Chelsea struggled against fury and a sense of betrayal. Uncle Bill was supposed to be her father's best friend. He stood by her father even when Aunt Brenda, his own sister, didn't believe in him. He'd known her father for longer than she'd been alive. If he didn't believe in her father's innocence, what chance did she have convincing anyone else? She couldn't remember ever feeling so alone.

"I need to go," she said, surging to her feet.

"Oh, Chelsea. Don't leave like this. I just don't want to see you get hurt."

"I've already been hurt. I have spent the last seven years without my dad. I've had to change my name in order to get the press to stop hounding me. My own aunt believes her brother is a murderer. Everyone has turned against Dad, but I won't. I know he loved Lily. He didn't kill her. And I'm going to prove it. To you. To everyone."

Chapter Ten

After dropping Chelsea at her house, Travis fought the Los Angeles traffic to the West Security and Investigations offices. He strode through the glass entrance and nearly ran into his boss.

"Just the man I was looking for," Kevin said with a smile.

"Really? You must have ESP."

"Well, I looked for you in your cubicle a moment ago. You weren't there, so I was headed out to grab a decent cup of coffee, but seeing as you're here now, it will just have to wait."

"You got something?" Travis asked, following Kevin across the polished tile floor to his office.

Kevin gave them a brief nod and kept walking. "How is Chelsea recovering from the hit-and-run?"

"Better than I'd be. She's still got some pain," Travis said, recalling the ibuprofen she'd swallowed with her coffee that morning, "but she's going to be fine. She's tough."

Kevin slid a sidelong glance at Travis, appraising him. "I have to agree. That was quite a tuck-and-roll she did to get out of the way of that car's path."

They stepped into Kevin's corner office. Light streamed in from the bay of windows. The office was decorated in a minimalist fashion that was simultaneously masculine with lots of dark wood and leather. Kevin's office was one of the largest on the floor, second only to Tess's. Dual sleek silver monitors sat on a desk. Kevin tapped on the keyboard, and the large flat screen mounted to the opposite wall glowed to life. A black-and-white image of the street a few yards from their office building appeared.

"We were able to get security footage from several of our neighbors," Kevin said. "You can take a look at all the tapes, seven in total that caught glimpses of the car that hit Chelsea. I've spliced them together to approximate the route the car took." He tapped the keyboard again, and the tape began. "There's the car. A late model sedan. It sits across the street there idling while Chelsea is inside our offices. It appears this guy followed her to her meeting with you."

The black Oldsmobile sat about twenty feet from the front of the West Investigations building. Waiting.

Travis hoped to see the outline of the driver, but he or she had the sunshade pulled down, covering the top of their face. The recording was too grainy and from too far of a distance to make out any distinguishing features on the driver.

He and Kevin watched as Chelsea walked out of the front of the building and started to cross the street. His body tensed, anticipating what was about to happen. The Oldsmobile pulled away from the curb as Chelsea stepped into the street and accelerated toward her. Travis's heart thundered, watching Chelsea turn toward the danger and freeze for a moment. Then she was in motion, running for the opposite sidewalk. The car swerved into her path. She leaped for the sidewalk as the right front side of the car clipped her hip. That leap had probably kept her from suffering far greater injuries. It may have even saved her life. Chelsea hit the pavement just short of the curb and rolled between two parked cars. The sedan sped off.

"Can you rewind the tape and slow it down? Focusing on the sedan's driver."

"I've pulled some still photos, but there hasn't been a good enough shot to get an identification," Kevin said while he rewound the video. He handed Travis the photos, but he was right. They were worthless.

They watched the video again at a slower pace, but the driver wore a baseball cap pulled low over his brow and sunglasses in addition to having used the sun visor to conceal his identity.

"Did any of the cameras get a shot of the license plates?" Kevin shook his head. "There were none."

Travis's stomach sank. The lack of license plates along with the driver's efforts to shield his identity confirmed what he already suspected. The hit-and-run hadn't been an accident. Someone had specifically targeted Chelsea. The still unanswered question was, had the driver meant to kill her or was this just a warning to back off investigating her father's case?

Either way, it meant Chelsea was in danger. It was impossible to believe that the hit-and-run wasn't connected to Chelsea's efforts to prove her father's innocence. Had Lily's killer somehow found out about Chelsea's investigation into the murder and decided to put a stop to it? If so, how had the killer learned about the investigation? There were dozens of names in Chelsea's binder, and Chelsea had said she'd reached out to several of Lily's friends and family before coming to him for help. Any one of them might want her to drop her investigation, either because they believed Franklin Brooks was in jail where he belonged or because they wanted to protect themselves or someone else. But right now, the hit-and-run driver appeared to be a dead end.

"Have we had any luck tracking down Peter Schmeichel?"

Kevin shook his head. "Peter doesn't appear to have a fixed address. I pulled his criminal record. It's as long as my arm, mostly drug offenses. A couple of assaults and batteries." He handed Travis a sheaf of papers. He hadn't been kidding about Peter's criminal history. The guy was a career criminal.

"Humph." Travis wasn't buying it. "What about locating Gina?"

"I've had better luck with that." Kevin tapped his keyboard, and Travis's phone chimed with the incoming text. "That's her current work and home address. She moved to San Bernardino about a year after Lily's death."

"This is great, thanks." Travis noted the address was about an hour away from Los Angeles. He could have just called Gina, but interviews were always more fruitful face-to-face. Plus, he wasn't convinced Gina had told the police everything she knew about Lily's murder. But she would tell him.

"Can you also check if Lily ever filed a police report for vandalism or a burglary at her place?" He explained what Rachel had told him and Chelsea, as well as the information that Jace, the neighbor, had given them about a possible new boyfriend.

"I'll see what I can do, but it might take a bit of time

to search police reports from seven-plus years ago that may or may not exist."

Travis's phone rang. He looked at the screen and saw the call was from Chelsea.

"Hello?"

"Did you call my aunt?" Chelsea asked without preamble.

"What? No, why?"

"I went to my uncle Bill's house—he's my dad's best friend—to ask him what he remembers about Lily and my dad's relationship, and my aunt called me as I was leaving. Someone called her asking a bunch of questions about me."

"You were supposed to be home resting," he said, tamping down his anger that she'd gone out alone.

"You said I should rest. I never agreed to it. Anyway, my aunt is more important."

"What kind of questions did the caller ask?" Travis said.

"I don't know," she answered, her voice rising. "Aunt Brenda said a man called saying he was a friend, and he asked questions about me and Dad. Then he said that it could be dangerous for me to continue on my quest to get Dad out of prison."

"The caller threatened you?" Travis growled.

"Not in so many words. I'm headed to my aunt's house now to check in on her."

"Send me her address," he said, already moving toward Kevin's office door.

"If you need any backup, give me a shout," Kevin said as he left.

Travis nodded to let Kevin know he heard him and

kept moving. His phone dinged in his ear. He pulled it away long enough to see that Chelsea had sent him her aunt's address.

"I'm on my way. I'll meet you there in twenty minutes," he said, racing from the office.

Chapter Eleven

He ate his lunch. A turkey sandwich on wheat, light mustard, heavy on the mayonnaise with a diet Coke. He ate alone as usual. His coworkers barely acknowledged him. He bet if asked most wouldn't even know his name. Some might not even recognize him if pressed. He knew how to blend in. How to go unnoticed. How to be unseen even when people were looking directly at him. That gave him space. To remember. To think. To plan.

She hadn't backed off after the hit-and-run. Chelsea Harper was tough, a fighter. Part of him admired her for it. But the other part, the bigger part, hated it. Hated her for making him feel this way. For turning him into a ball of nerves. For making him sneak around, hiding in the shadows, jumping at every shape and sound.

This would not do.

She was going to cause trouble, he knew it. But he couldn't just get rid of her.

She was going to keep asking questions. Ask even more questions, better questions, now that she'd hired a private detective. Dammit to hell and back.

Why wouldn't she just give up investigating Lily's case? Everyone else had. The whole world was convinced that Franklin Brooks killed Lily Wong. They'd convicted him and thrown away the key. No one cared anymore. No one except Franklin Brooks's daughter.

She was bringing it all back to the forefront of everyone's mind. What if someone remembered seeing him? What if that drugged-out fool grew a conscience? Admitted he'd lied? What if Chelsea and her private investigator succeeded in getting the police and prosecutor to reopen Franklin's case?

He couldn't let that happen. Too bad just killing her wasn't an option. But that would surely attract more attention than he wanted. Franklin Brooks's daughter getting killed when she was pressing for his case to be reopened. Shouting from the rafters to anyone who would listen that her father was innocent. The cops wouldn't be able to just write it off as coincidence.

He wasn't sure what it would take to get her to back off, but he had to figure it out.

He had to stop her.

He'd made it this long without anyone suspecting him. He didn't intend to go to jail.

Chapter Twelve

Chelsea pulled into her aunt's driveway just as Travis pulled to a stop in front of the house. She didn't slow down to let him catch up with her as she headed to the front door. The door opened as she lifted her hand to knock.

"Aunt Brenda, are you okay?" Chelsea let her gaze roam over her aunt from head to toe.

Aunt Brenda was a willowy woman with dark brown hair that had gone mostly gray and keen hazel eyes. She'd had surgery on her knees two years earlier that had left her with a slight limp, but she kept in shape by swimming regularly at the local recreation center.

"Of course I'm okay. You don't think a little old phone call is going to do me in, do you?"

"Well, no," Chelsea said, "but you seemed upset."

"I was upset for you, not me." Aunt Brenda leaned to her right, looking around Chelsea. "Who's he?"

Chelsea glanced over her shoulder at Travis, who was standing several feet behind her. His eyes swept over the street before coming back to land on her and her aunt. "This is Travis Collins, the private investigator I hired to help me get Dad out of jail."

Her aunt's face twisted into a scowl. "Waste of time and money if you ask me."

She hadn't asked, and it was her money, Chelsea thought, but she bit back that retort.

"Ladies, might I suggest we take this discussion inside?" Travis nodded toward the interior of the house.

Her aunt's scowl deepened, but she stood aside and let Chelsea and Travis in. The door snapped closed behind them, and Aunt Brenda turned, crossing her arms over her chest. "Is he the friend who called me?"

"No," Chelsea said through gritted teeth. "We don't know who called you. That's what we are hoping to find out."

"Chelsea, you know I try to put your father and all that nastiness that came with his trial behind me. I don't want to dredge all that up. I would think that you'd feel the same way. Picking at this scab could ruin your life."

Chelsea took a deep breath. Her aunt looked so much like her father, especially when she was mad, it was hard to look at her and not see him. In some ways, it was comforting, like still having a piece of her father with her. In others, it made her yearn for all that she had lost. "Seeking the truth is not going to ruin my life."

Aunt Brenda threw her hands up in the air and stomped past Chelsea and Travis into the kitchen. "Well, I want no part of it. Tell your friend never to call me again."

"Aunt Brenda, you aren't listening. I didn't tell anyone to call you."

"I don't understand you." Aunt Brenda looked around the kitchen as if understanding might be hiding on top of a cabinet or behind the toaster. "Why can't you just go on with your life? Forget about your father. Find a nice guy to settle down with and have a family of your own."

"I have a family. You, Victor, Uncle Bill and Dad." Chelsea emphasized her last word.

Her aunt let out a sigh of frustration, but her eyes were tinged with fear. "If you dredge this up again, people may realize who you are. Who your father is. What will they think of you?"

"I don't care what people think about me."

"That's obvious," her aunt shot back.

This was an argument they'd had dozens of times before, and neither was going to give in to the other. It wasn't why Chelsea had come to her aunt's house, either, so it was best to move on.

"On the phone, you said that the person who called was a man. Did he give you a name?" Chelsea asked.

Aunt Brenda shook her head, her expression contemplative. "I don't think so. He just said he was a friend of yours."

"Did the call come in on your home phone or your cell phone?" Travis asked.

Aunt Brenda nodded to the black handset and cradle on the kitchen counter. "Home. I hardly bother with that cell. Only a few people even have the number."

"Do you mind if I take a look at the incoming call log?" Travis asked.

"Knock yourself out."

"How long ago did you get the call?" Travis reached for the handset and pressed a button.

"Maybe an hour ago." Aunt Brenda glanced at the clock on the microwave. "I called Chelsea right after."

"Can you remember anything else about the call?" Chelsea asked, pulling her attention back to her. "Background noises? Did the man have an accent? Anything you remember could help us identify him."

"I don't know, Chels. It was a regular call." Her aunt

grabbed a dishrag from the sink and wiped haphazardly at the counter.

Chelsea knew her aunt cleaned when she was worried. She felt a moment's guilt for being the cause of that worry, but not enough to stop investigating.

"He said he was a friend of yours and that he knew we were investigating your father's case," Aunt Brenda continued. "He was concerned that you were in over your head. Those were his exact words, in over your head and that you could get hurt." Aunt Brenda scrubbed at a mark that had been on the counter for as long as Chelsea could remember.

She reached out and covered her aunt's hand with her own, stilling it.

Aunt Brenda's gaze met hers. "I asked what he meant by saying you could get hurt, but he just hung up."

Chelsea pulled her aunt into a hug. "I'm not going to get hurt."

"The number the call came in from was blocked," Travis said, replacing the phone on its cradle.

Chelsea pulled back from the embrace with her aunt but kept one arm around the older woman. "Now what?"

"Now you stop this madness." Her aunt shrugged out from under Chelsea's arm. "I've already lost a brother and a husband. I won't lose you, too."

"You won't lose me," Chelsea said.

"No?" her aunt spat angrily. "You think I don't know what's going on here? That call was a warning. A threat."

Another stab of guilt cut through Chelsea. She hadn't told her aunt about the hit-and-run earlier because she didn't want to worry her. But now didn't seem like a good time to tell her, either.

"I'm sorry, Aunt Brenda, but I have to do this. I'll be

careful, and I have Travis to help me. He's a former cop and a private investigator. We've already turned up some good leads that the police didn't follow up on seven years ago. I'll be careful, I promise."

Her aunt shook her head, a single tear falling over the crest of her cheek. "I can't talk you out of this, but I won't be a part of it." She turned and rushed from the room. A moment later the sound of a bedroom door slamming carried into the kitchen.

Chelsea let out a heavy sigh.

"She loves you," Travis said, coming to stand next to Chelsea.

"I know."

His voice lowered. "She's not wrong about the potential danger."

Chelsea studied him. "Did you learn something at West's offices this afternoon?"

"We probably shouldn't talk about it here." Travis had a look down the hallway where her aunt had disappeared.

"Come on. I haven't eaten since breakfast, and I'm starved," Chelsea said. "You can tell me the bad news over food."

"Do you have any particular place in mind?"

Chelsea flashed a weary smile. "My favorite place isn't too far. Follow me."

Chapter Thirteen

"Eight fish tacos coming up." The teen behind the food truck window shot a toothy grin at Chelsea as she passed him the cash for the food. He made change and handed it back to her.

"This is your favorite place to eat?" Travis asked when they stepped back to wait for their food.

"One of them, yes." She held up a finger. "It's afford-able. The tacos are the best on the West Coast." She held up a second finger. "And the views can't be beat." She spread out a hand to encompass the waves lapping against the sands of El Segundo Beach. Tucked under her other arm was the blanket she kept in the trunk of her car.

The views were spectacular, which was why this was one of her favorite places on earth, even with the crush of people mobbing the shoreline along the water.

"Eight fish tacos," the teen called out.

Chelsea grinned up at Travis. "And the service is quick," she added, walking back to the food truck to grab their order. She handed the bag of food and two canned iced teas to Travis.

At the edge of the beach, they shucked their shoes, and Chelsea carried them and the blanket down the beach until they found a spot that was not as crowded. She spread the blanket out over the flat sand, and they sat down.

"Do you do this often?" Travis asked. "Dine on the beach?"

Chelsea handed him two tacos. "I spent a lot of time here with my dad when I was growing up. It's not too far from Aunt Brenda's place, and it's cheap, so it fit right into our budget."

Travis unwrapped one of the tacos and ate half of it in one bite. "It must have been nice to have a beach so close to home."

"It was great. I take it you didn't grow up in Los Angeles."

Travis shook his head. "I grew up in the Midwest." He didn't give her any more information, instead stuffing the remaining portion of the taco in his mouth.

"I like to come here and think. After my dad was arrested, it was one of the only places I could go for a while where people didn't recognize me. I could blend into the crowd of beachgoers."

"It must have been hard for you after your father was arrested."

"It's like everyone—not just the cops, but my friends, my aunt—everyone believed that my dad did it. And because I didn't, I became one of the bad guys, too."

"I'm sorry."

Chelsea took a bite of taco, chewed and swallowed. "Victor was really the only person to stand by me. I mean, I know he thinks my dad is where he belongs, but he doesn't treat me any differently than he did before." She brought the iced tea to her lips.

"Victor?"

"My cousin. More like my brother. He's my aunt Brenda and uncle Darren's only child. We grew up together."

"Is he in one of the photos on your dresser?"

Chelsea made a face. "My dresser?"

"I noticed the photos that you have on top when I went to the bathroom at your place yesterday. I didn't go into your room," he added quickly. "I promise."

"Oh, yeah, that's Victor."

"Your cousin." Something passed over Travis's face.

"Yes. My cousin. Why?"

"Nothing. I just thought he might be a boyfriend."

She laughed. "You met Simon, so you know my track record with men isn't good. I haven't even had a date in, I don't remember how long."

He wiped his hands on a napkin, but not before Chelsea saw a satisfied smile on his face. Wait… He'd thought Victor was her boyfriend, and now that he knew he wasn't, was he happy she was single? Maybe he'd even been a little jealous. The idea of it made her insides do a happy dance before she reminded herself they could only have a business relationship.

Travis cleared his throat. "Listen, I wanted to tell you what the team at West has been able to turn up." Whatever he might have been thinking or feeling, it was gone, replaced by his usual professionalism.

She sighed internally, wiped her own hands on a napkin and set her iced tea to the side. "Great. Shoot."

"We got video of the hit-and-run from the businesses surrounding the office. This was no accident, Chelsea. The driver followed you to the office and waited for you to come out. He never swerved. In fact, he aimed for you."

Travis's words stole her breath. She'd suspected the hit-and-run wasn't an accident, but to have it confirmed was to face the fact that someone out there wanted to hurt her. Badly.

Travis put a hand on her arm. "Are you okay?"

Chelsea nodded slowly. "Yeah, just processing."

"We weren't able to get a good look at the driver's face or the tags on the car, but we know to watch out for a black sedan now."

"Okay," Chelsea said on a long breath.

"And this might be a good time to mention how bad an idea it was to sneak off to speak with your uncle earlier—"

Chelsea scowled. "I didn't sneak anywhere. I'm a grown woman. I can go where I please."

He held up his hands. "*Sneak* was the wrong word. But that hit-and-run was intentional. You need to be careful. At least let me know your plans so I can have your back even if I disagree with them."

She felt her ire dissipate. "Okay. I'll keep you in the loop from now on."

"Great. Now, can I ask what you and your uncle discussed?"

She filled him in on the conversation with her uncle. "Unfortunately, he didn't remember anything that could help us."

"Well, I do have some good news. We got an address for Gina. She's living in San Bernardino now."

"That's great. Are you going to give her a call or—"

"I was thinking we could take a trip up there and talk to her in person."

"Even better. Let's go," Chelsea said, starting to push to her feet.

Travis laid a hand on her arm again, keeping her on the blanket. "Slow down. I have to get some things in order first. Gina is working as a nurse at a local hospital. I don't want to have to ambush her at her job, so I need to try to get her schedule to see if we can catch her at home."

Frustration bubbled in Chelsea's chest, but she'd hired Travis for his help so she needed to take it. "Whatever you think is the best plan, I'm on board. When do you want to go?"

"I'm thinking about tomorrow afternoon."

Chelsea collected their trash and stuffed it into the taco bag. This time when she stood, Travis stood with her. Her feet sank into the sand and combined with her excitement and haste, she lost her footing.

Travis grabbed her, his hands winding around her waist, steadying her against his hard body. She angled her head to look up at him and saw desire in his eyes. The same desire that she felt.

Travis sucked in a breath that made her knees go weak again. He bought his mouth down, nearly touching hers. They stood there a moment, hovering at the edge of an invisible line.

A shriek ripped through the air a moment before a young girl came tearing down the sand.

Travis's arms dropped from her waist, and he took three large steps back. "I should get you home." He turned away, bending down to collect the blanket and their shoes.

Chelsea let out the breath she'd been holding. The young girl's parents ambled by, their arms loaded down with stuff, completely oblivious to the moment they'd interrupted.

But it was good that they'd been interrupted. She and Travis were obviously attracted to each other, but crossing the line could have repercussions neither of them needed at the moment. But now she just had to figure out a way to forget how she felt in his arms.

THAT WAS A near miss, Travis thought as he followed Chelsea to make sure she got home without incident. He'd almost kissed her. The way she'd melted against him had almost made him forget that she was a client. And that he didn't do relationships. He also knew Chelsea wasn't the kind of woman who did casual relationships. Luckily, that screaming kid had come along and brought him back to his senses. As soon as he was sure Chelsea was safe and sound inside her house, he'd head home and take a long cold shower and pretend nothing had happened.

He pulled into Chelsea's driveway behind her car and got out.

"I'm fine, Travis. You don't have to see me to my door."

He stopped next to her. "I do, actually. I promised your dad I'd watch out for you, and I mean to keep that promise."

"Fine," she huffed, turning and marching to her porch. She opened her front door and froze.

Travis immediately grabbed her and moved her behind him so he was between her and the interior of the house. It looked like a cyclone had blown through her living room. Bloodred paint splattered the soft gray walls and just about everything else in the living room. A single word—*Stop*—had been written across one wall, red paint dripping down from each letter like a horror movie.

"Stay here," he ordered before entering the house. He swept through the living room, dining room and kitchen as well as the bedrooms. They'd all been trashed, but only the living room had been splattered with paint.

He returned to the doorway to find that Chelsea had ignored his admonishment to stay outside. She reached for the wall.

"Don't touch anything," he began, but her fingertips were already covered in paint.

"He did this. The man who called my aunt and tried to run me over," she said, sounding as if she was in a daze. He recognized that she was in shock. "The man who killed Lily."

Travis strode over to her, tilting her chin until she was looking at him, really looking at him. "We're going to get this guy. I promise you." He took her into his arms, not caring if it was professional or not. Her home had been invaded and violated, and she needed comfort. Hell, he could use a little comfort himself. When he first stepped up to the door and saw all that red, he'd thought…

Of course, that was what this psycho wanted. To scare Chelsea. Scare her enough that she'd back off. Her home looked like the site of a grisly murder.

"Let's go outside, and I'll call the police." He led her back to his car and got her safely inside before bypassing 911 and punching a familiar number into his cell. Less than ten minutes later, a gold sedan screeched to a stop behind his car.

Travis stretched out his hand toward the man who approached. Detective Gabe Owens was the only person from his police days that he kept in touch with, and only sparingly. Owens had joined the LAPD a couple of years after Travis and had still been in uniform when Travis left the force. That was probably the only reason Owens hadn't shunned him like the rest of his former colleagues. He'd still been idealistic enough to believe that Travis had done the right thing.

But it had been over a year since he and Owens had last grabbed a drink together. Gabe had aged, as they all had. The flaming red hair Travis remembered was more orange now, at least the part that hadn't completely turned gray. But more than anything it was Owens's eyes that had changed. He had the eyes now of a man who had seen too much.

"Hey, thanks for getting here so quickly," Travis said.

"No problem. I wasn't far. So, you said someone vandalized your friend's home."

"My client," he responded automatically, then remembering their near kiss, he added, "and friend kind of."

Owens shot him a knowing look. "Okay, tell me about this client/friend kind of."

Travis shoved off the embarrassing description of Chelsea and gave Owens a quick rundown of the investigation, the recent threats against her life and now her coming home to a paint-splattered mess.

"You always did like the complicated ones," Owens said.

Travis wasn't sure whether Owens was referring to cases or women. He wasn't sure he wanted to know.

Owens insisted on clearing the house himself. Travis and Chelsea waited on the front step until he returned.

"It doesn't look like anything was stolen, but would you come inside and have a look?" Owens asked Chelsea.

Travis and Chelsea followed Owens back into the house. The way the place had been trashed, but it didn't seem like the perp had been looking for anything in particular. He'd just been bent on destruction. The televisions in the living room and Chelsea's bedroom had been smashed as had most of her china and several lamps. Her clothes were thrown around her bedroom, some clearly destroyed, and nearly every cabinet and drawer had been pulled out and their contents dumped. The papers Chelsea had collected in her investigation had been torn to shreds and littered the dining room floor.

"Where's your binder, Chelsea?" Travis asked.

"My binder—" Chelsea looked at him for a moment, confused, until understanding took over. "Oh, thankfully I had one in my car with me, but I think I left the second one on the dining room table."

Travis followed her around the house, an arm that he hoped was comforting around her shoulders. Finally, they returned to where Owens stood, making notes for the incident report, in the living room.

"It's hard to tell for sure," Chelsea said, "but I don't think anything is missing, just destroyed." She pointed to the dining room where the files she'd compiled on her father's case had been ripped and torn to shreds.

"Do you have any idea who could have done this? An ex-boyfriend?" Owens glanced at Travis. "A current boyfriend?"

Travis caught the look Chelsea shot at him before she answered, "Not exactly."

Owens's bushy brows rose. "What does that mean, exactly?"

"My ex-husband paid me an unexpected visit the other day, but I don't think he would do something like this."

Travis had taken an instant dislike to the man, but he had to agree with Chelsea. Whoever had done this had exhibited a lot of uncontrolled rage. Simon seemed like the type of guy who wouldn't have wanted to muss his hair. But looks could be deceiving, so he was glad Owens insisted on taking Simon's information down. Travis would also be checking into Simon more closely, something he should have thought of earlier.

"Can you think of anyone else who may be angry with you?" Owens asked Chelsea.

Chelsea shot Travis a look that seemed to say *where do I start?*

Travis stepped in, adding more detail to the brief explanation he'd given Owens outside. He explained Chelsea's theory that her father was innocent of the murder he was in jail for and that they were revisiting the case.

"And you think whoever did those things did this?" Owens summarized.

"Who else?" Chelsea responded sharply.

"I'm just trying to understand, Ms. Harper."

"I think it's the obvious answer, Owens," Travis seconded.

"And you think that person also really killed Lily Wong?" Owens asked.

"Yes," Chelsea answered definitively.

At the same time Travis said, "We don't know."

Chelsea shot him a look that would have turned him to dust if it could have.

Travis knew she thought her father's innocence was an absolute certainty, but he still had questions. Someone clearly wanted her to stop investigating, but that didn't mean that person was Lily Wong's true killer. It was just as possible that someone didn't appreciate Chelsea making waves.

Owens gave them both a long look. "Well, we don't usually dust for prints when nothing has been taken, but as a courtesy to you, Trav, I can have the boys come out. It may take them several hours to get here, though."

"Thanks," Travis responded. "I appreciate it."

"I'll write up the incident report. You need it to file a claim with your insurance company for the damages and replace your things."

"Thanks," Chelsea responded.

"Do you have a place to stay until the lock gets fixed?" Owens asked.

"She will be fine," Travis interjected before Chelsea spoke. "I'll take care of it."

Chelsea shot him a second disgruntled look.

"Here's my card." Owens handed a card to Chelsea. "I'll have the report ready for you in a couple days. You can call me directly if you have any more trouble."

"Thank you," Chelsea repeated, this time in a voice so small it tore through Travis. She didn't deserve this. To have her home violated in this way.

Owens started for the door, and Travis followed him outside. "Owens, look, I know I'm not a favorite citizen of the LAPD—"

Owens held up a meaty hand. "Look, man, you did what you felt was right. I respect that."

Travis was surprised. It had been some time since he'd spoken to a former colleague. At best he'd been treated like a pariah after he turned several of his colleagues into internal affairs for evidence tampering. At worst, he'd fielded threats that had him sleeping with his gun by his side. No one had ever indicated they believed he'd done the right thing by turning his colleagues in. "Thanks."

He said goodbye and went back inside the house.

"You can't stay here tonight," he said as Chelsea picked up the shattered remnants of a photograph of her and her aunt.

"Where else am I going to go?"

"You can get a hotel room."

She let out a strangled laugh. "You're kidding. I live on a teacher's salary. I can barely afford my mortgage and I've had to cut back in order to pay West's fee, and I can't leave with the lock smashed in like that."

"I can fix the lock, temporarily at least. But it's too dangerous for you to be here. Whoever is doing this is currently escalating. You shouldn't go anywhere alone until we find this guy and put him behind bars." He hesitated for a moment, considering the idea he'd been tossing around in his head. "You could stay with me. I have a spare room."

Chelsea studied him. "What did you mean when you said you didn't know if the person who did this is the person who killed Lily? You can't possibly believe all this—" she spread her arms out encompassing the destruction in the house "—isn't related to her death."

"It's definitely related, but we have no proof that the person who is doing this is Lily's killer."

"You still think my dad did it, don't you?"

"I haven't made any conclusions yet."

Chelsea stared at him for another long moment before turning and starting down the hall toward her bedroom.

"Chelsea, you might be angry with me now, but your safety—"

"I'm not stupid or foolhardy, Travis. I'll take you up on your offer of your spare bedroom."

He breathed out a sigh of relief.

"I'm going to see if I have enough undamaged clothes to pack a bag," she said, still not looking at him. "You should be able to find something to keep the door closed until I can get a locksmith here."

He watched her disappear into her bedroom, all the while something tugged at his insides. He was losing the battle to ignore his growing feelings for Chelsea. And even scarier, he was realizing that he wasn't sure it was a battle he really wanted to fight.

Chapter Fourteen

The next morning, Chelsea blinked her eyes open, her heart racing as she took in the unfamiliar room, then settled when she remembered where she was. In Travis's guestroom. In Travis's apartment. Because her home was not safe. Although the temperature in the room was a tad on the warm side, a chill went through her.

Travis had shored up her front door enough that it would hold for a night as long as the vandal didn't return to inflict more damage. She glanced at the clock on the nightstand—8:00 a.m. She'd slept later than usual.

She supposed she shouldn't be surprised. The day before had been long and trying, and she'd spent an hour after Travis got her settled in the guest room searching Lily's dormant social media pages for any hint of her mystery boyfriend, to no avail. It was enough to make her contemplate pulling the covers up over her head and hiding. One day in bed, a very comfortable one at that, was that too much to ask? But she had too much to do to hide out, no matter how much she wanted to or how enticing the mattress was.

She took a quick shower, then gathered her hair into a bun. Efficiency was going to have to trump fashion until she was back in her own place with all of her own things.

She slipped on a pair of black slacks, a burgundy knit top and black ankle boots. As she stepped out of the guest room, she smelled coffee and sautéed onions.

She found Travis in front of the stove making omelets. His back was to her. He wore a pair of gray sweatpants that clung to well-shaped buttocks. A black T-shirt stretched over the muscles of his arms and back. She allowed herself a moment to take him in completely before reminding herself that romance wasn't in the cards for them, no matter how delectable the man whose house she was now sharing. She gave herself a shake and entered the kitchen.

"Good morning," she said as she walked over to the coffee pot.

"Good morning," Travis responded without turning. "The omelets are almost done."

Chelsea poured herself a cup, adding cream and sugar, which Travis had already placed next to the carafe. She turned to find him staring at her. "Is everything okay?"

Travis blinked and turned back to the omelets. "Yeah, these are done. Have a seat."

Chelsea sat at the kitchen table, contemplating the look she'd seen on Travis's face. It was almost as if the sight of her had stunned him speechless. But that couldn't be, could it? He had been the one to pull away from her the day before at the beach. She was sure he'd been about to kiss her, and she would have let him. Heck, she wanted him to kiss her. As much as she'd tried to keep things professional between them, there was undeniably an attraction there.

Travis slid an omelet onto the plate in front of her.

"This looks great," she said as he slid a second omelet onto the plate across from hers.

He put the pan back on the stove and took his seat. "Thanks," he said. "I'm not much for cooking, but as I said, I can handle breakfast and a few simple meals."

She took a bite. "This *is* great. You can be in charge of breakfast every morning as far as I'm concerned." Heat rose in her cheeks as she realized what she'd implied. That they would be having breakfast together every morning. Hopefully, she'd be able to get a locksmith to her house today, and this would be the only time they had breakfast together. The thought made her sad.

They ate in silence for a few minutes. Finally, Travis spoke up. "I got Gina's schedule at the hospital. She works the 9:00 p.m. to 9:00 a.m. shift. I thought we could drive out to speak with her after we get your door fixed."

"That's great, but I haven't even contacted a locksmith yet."

"I hope you don't mind," he said. "I contacted the locksmith that West Investigations keeps on retainer. He'll meet us at your place whenever you're ready."

"That's great. Thank you. Could you arrange for him to come by this morning? Detective Owens left me a voicemail while I was in the shower to say he'd finished dusting my house for fingerprints, so I can get out of your hair today."

"You're welcome. And you're not in my hair. Actually, I wanted to talk to you about staying here for a few more days."

"Staying here?"

"We could stay at your place, but I do think you'd be safer here. For one thing, I have a security system, and you don't."

"Wait. Slow down. Why would I need to stay here or you stay with me if I change the locks?"

"Even with your locks changed, you'll still be in danger. I don't think it's safe for you to be at your place. Or alone generally."

"I can't hide."

"I know. And I'm not asking you to. Staying with me or me staying with you at your place would be a deterrent to whoever has been targeting you. They know someone has your back."

"You?"

"Me."

Warmth spread through her. "It still feels like hiding. I don't like the idea of being run out of my own home."

"I can understand that, but think of it more as taking precautions. Not running or hiding."

She raised her coffee mug to her lips, thinking. There was some validity to what Travis said. If someone broke into her home again, having Travis there would certainly be better than being alone. And she had to admit, as much as she wanted to go home, she was still a little afraid. A couple more days in Travis's bed wouldn't be a hardship. *In Travis's guest bed*, she mentally amended. Alone. Her cheeks heated again, and she fought the urge to fan herself.

"Okay. Um, I'll stay here."

He smiled. "Great."

"Great." She brought the coffee mug to her lips again.

"I'd like to take you out to dinner tonight."

Chelsea spat coffee onto what was left of her omelet. Travis rounded the table but paused when she held out her hand to stop him. She was embarrassed enough. She didn't need him patting her back like a father trying to burp an infant. She caught her breath enough to sputter, "Dinner?"

"Yes. I would like to take you to dinner." He handed her a napkin.

She wiped at the coffee dripping down her chin. "Why?"

"Because you've made dinner and showed me where I can get the best fish tacos on the West Coast. I'd like to do something nice for you. And you mentioned it had been a while since you went out for a nice meal."

Oh, so that was it. He felt sorry for her. "You don't have to do that."

One of his shoulders rose in a shrug. "I know I don't have to. I want to." He picked up his plate and carried it to the sink before turning back to her. "It's just dinner. We have to eat, and it's not fair for you to do all the heavy lifting. I can't cook dinner, but I'm a champ at paying for it," he joked.

That got a smile from her. Why not? He was right. It was just dinner. Dinner with a colleague, kind of. They were working together, after all. *And living together for the moment*, a little voice chimed in. She ignored it. "Okay. Yes. I'd like to go to dinner with you."

Travis's shoulders relaxed. "Tonight then. Meet you in the living room at 8:00 p.m."

A tingling sensation ignited her body. It had been a long time since she'd been on a date. Even if it was just a friendly dinner date. After she cleared her father and got him out of prison, she would get a life. Aunt Brenda was right about how Chelsea should find someone to settle down with and start a family. Someone better for her than Simon ever was.

Her gaze went to Travis, who was still looking at her in a way that made her pulse pound. Places inside her that had long been dormant awakened.

Whoa, girl. She didn't need to ask to know he wasn't the settling-down type, but her body didn't seem to have gotten that message. Luckily, her brain was still in control. She wanted a real connection with someone, not just a roll in the sack. Not that rolling around with Travis wouldn't be fun. She was pretty sure he would be extraordinary in bed. But the moment would be fleeting. She didn't need the additional emotional drama that playing with a man like him was sure to cause.

No. Friends were all she and Travis could ever be. And she'd keep saying that for as long as it took her to believe it.

Chapter Fifteen

Travis helped her straighten up her house as much as they could while the locksmith fixed her door. Dealing with the paint-splattered walls would take more effort and lots of primer, but she was glad Travis had offered to help. Even though she'd agreed to stay with him for a few days, she felt an urgency to erase the vandal's presence from her home.

The locksmith was not only good at his job, he was also fast. It took him less than an hour to change the locks and add a dead bolt at Travis's request. She had to admit the dead bolt did make her feel safer. She hoped the hesitance she felt being in her own home would pass quickly.

After she paid the locksmith, they headed to Gina's address.

Gina worked the nine-to-nine overnight shift, and when they pulled into her street a little after eleven o'clock, they saw a woman in blue scrubs matching her general description just getting out of a car parked in the driveway.

Chelsea and Travis headed up the concrete walkway to the front porch.

Gina turned toward them, a mask of distrust on her face.

"Gina McGrath," Chelsea said when they reached her, giving her a smile.

Gina's gaze cut to Travis, then back to Chelsea. "Who's asking?"

"My name is Chelsea Harper. This is Travis Collins. We are investigators."

"Investigators? What do you want with me?" Gina was dressed in scrubs, but even with their loose fit, Chelsea could see the woman was painfully thin. Gina's eyes were sunken, and her muddy brown hair was short and straight. Her lips were covered in bright red lipstick. She looked older than her forty-something years.

"We're looking into Lily Wong's murder. We understand you used to be her neighbor."

The frown on Gina's face hardened. "That was a long time ago. I told the police everything I know. I don't have anything more to say."

"We aren't with the police," Travis said. "We're conducting a separate investigation."

"Evidence has come to light suggesting Franklin Brooks may not have committed the murder," Chelsea added.

The comment clearly surprised Gina. She let the bag of groceries slide through her hands. Two apples rolled in opposite directions across the porch floor.

Travis went after them and handed the apples back to Gina.

"Thank you," she said, placing them in the bag again.

"If we can just speak to you for a moment," Travis said, trying again. "Please, it could help free an innocent man."

Gina hesitated for a long moment. "Come on in." She stepped back, allowing Chelsea and Travis to walk into the house, then closed the door and headed to the kitchen. She set the groceries on the counter and took a carton of milk from the bag. She put it in the fridge, then turned to face them, wariness in her eyes. "What kind of questions do you want to ask me?"

"We want to know about the night Lily died."

She reached into the grocery bag and pulled out a loaf of bread, not looking at either Travis or Chelsea. "Like I said, I already told the police everything I knew."

"We understand that, but sometimes things come back to us later. Details that we don't remember right away," Travis said.

Gina sighed. "I don't think I'll ever forget anything about that night. You don't forget the details of the day your neighbor was murdered."

"Can you tell us about it?" Travis asked.

Gina sighed a second time. "I got home from work late. Peter was there. I'd stupidly given him a key, which he took as an invitation to essentially move in. The house was a mess. I remember garbage day was the next day, and Peter hadn't taken the trash out. We argued about it, and I eventually ended up taking it out. That's when I saw Lily and Frank. They were on her front stoop talking."

"On the front stoop. Not in the house?" Chelsea said.

"On the stoop. They weren't arguing or anything, at least not that I could hear, but it kind of looked like Lily didn't want to let him in the house." She shrugged. "That's the vibe I got anyway."

"Why did you get this vibe?" Travis asked.

"I don't know. It was the way she was standing. Like right in front of it like she was blocking it so he couldn't come inside. Like with her arms crossed."

Gina looked at Chelsea for understanding. She got it. Arms crossed, defenses up, the universal signal among women that they weren't interested in whatever the man in front of them was saying at the moment.

"Like I said, it was just a feeling I got."

"So, you definitely didn't see Frank go into the house," Chelsea pressed.

Gina shook her head. "I can't say for sure they didn't go inside, but I didn't see them go inside."

"And Peter didn't go outside with you? You're sure about that."

"I'm sure."

Chelsea cut a glance at Travis. That confirmed the contradiction of Peter's statement at trial and at least suggested that the writer of the note was telling the truth. "In his testimony at trial, Peter said he took out the trash that night. That's when he supposedly saw Frank and Lily arguing and Frank follow Lily into the house," Travis said.

Gina reached into the grocery bag, avoiding their gazes again. She turned her back on them, putting canned peaches into an overhead cabinet.

"Gina, was Peter in the house or not?" Travis asked softly.

"He never left the sofa that night. I'm not a liar." Her back stayed to them.

"But Peter is?"

Gina turned and looked at them. "Peter had problems back then."

"He was arrested for possession about a week after Lily's murder. Carrying enough drugs to have been charged with a felony," Travis said. "It would have been his third strike, which meant he was in danger of serving serious time behind bars."

Gina didn't respond.

"So maybe Peter saw an opportunity," Chelsea picked up the narrative. "Tell the cops what they want to hear about Frank and Lily, and they'd look the other way regarding his charges."

"I don't know anything about that," Gina said, still avoiding looking directly at them.

"But you suspect," Travis pressed her.

Gina flattened her lips into a thin line but stayed quiet.

Chelsea moved across the kitchen and stood directly in front of the woman. "Gina, I'm not just doing this to right a wrong. Franklin Brooks is my father. He has spent the last seven years of his life in jail separated from his family who loves him because of a lie."

Gina sighed and finally looked Chelsea in the eye. "I don't know anything for a fact, but I told the cops the truth. I didn't know about what Peter told them until later. They believed him over me, and the cop seemed pretty sure that Franklin killed Lily so—"

"So, you just left it," Chelsea said, unable to curtail the hint of anger in her tone.

"What was I supposed to do?" Gina challenged. "The cops had their killer."

"Let's stay focused on the night Lily died, okay?" Travis interjected. "Did you see Franklin leave Lily's house that night?" he asked Gina.

"No," she responded.

"Did you notice anything or hear anything at all unusual after you saw Lily and Franklin?"

Gina scrunched her face as if she was thinking. After a beat, she responded, "Unusual, no. I put the trash out by the curb, waved at Lily and she waved back."

"Wait a minute." Travis said. "Did you see Jace Orson? He said he was out with friends the night Lily was killed."

Gina laughed. "Jace? Out? With friends? No way. If

he wasn't at work, he was at home, and I'm pretty sure he didn't have any friends."

"That's what he told us," Travis said.

"Well, then he lied. He was definitely home and I saw him."

There was no mention of Gina having seen Jace in her statement.

"Did you tell the cops about seeing Jace that night?" Travis asked.

"I don't know. I don't think so. They were mostly focused on the argument I had seen between Lily and Franklin."

"Do you have any idea where we can find Peter now?" Chelsea asked.

"Last I heard he'd moved to Monterey, but that was eons ago. I haven't seen or heard from him in years. And good riddance."

They thanked Gina and headed back to the car.

"We need to find Peter and talk to Jace Orson again," Chelsea said as they fastened their seat belts.

Travis flashed her a grim smile. "You read my mind."

Chapter Sixteen

Chelsea Harper just would not back down. He'd watched her house. Seen the locksmith come to fix the door. Watched through the windows as she and the private investigator cleaned up inside. He had a clear view into the house now since he'd slashed the curtains and pulled them from the wall.

It looked like they were pretty cozy with each other. Downright domestic. Maybe the obvious attraction between the two would distract Chelsea from her investigation.

He didn't hold out much hope for that, but women were fickle. Lily had proven that, hadn't she? She'd left Franklin, and then—just when he'd been about to make his move, to show her the right man for her was right in front of her—she took up with that other guy. The memory of seeing her with the new guy sat like a stone in his gut. It still made him want to scream at times.

The memories of Lily both comforted and tormented him. He hadn't meant to kill her. He'd wanted her. He'd loved her. He still did. His stomach churned. Things had just gotten out of control. *He'd* gotten out of control. He had only been trying to make her understand. Understand that they were meant to be together. But it had all gone so wrong.

He'd hoped that Chelsea could be easily scared off her investigation. But when he'd seen her dining room, her research, everything she'd collected on her father's case, he'd known that would never happen. And then they'd gone and tracked down Gina.

This had the potential to be bad. Really bad. Chelsea would keep digging until she found the truth. Until she found him.

He knew what it would take to get her to stop now. But it was dangerous, too dangerous. He shouldn't even be thinking about it, but he was. He had always hoped it wouldn't come to this, but he'd also known that if it did, he'd do what needed to be done.

It seemed like the time had come.

His rage boiled, stoked by once again being forced to do something he didn't want to do. Forced to lose control.

He needed to get out of here before he did something stupid. He'd do what he had to do, but he needed to think. To plan. Whatever he did, it couldn't come back on him. He didn't want the authorities to even think of his name in relation to Chelsea Harper's.

He started the engine and pressed the accelerator. He needed to think. He had to figure out how to stop Chelsea and the private investigator before they ruined everything.

Chapter Seventeen

Jace Orson didn't answer the door at his house when Chelsea and Travis dropped by. Travis had used West's resources to dig up a phone number for him, but Jace hadn't answered his call, either. That, and Gina's surety that Jace had been home the night of Lily's murder, was enough to make Chelsea want to track him down and force the truth out of him immediately.

But Travis pointed out that they had no power to force anything out of anyone. They weren't the police. And Jace not being at home didn't really mean anything anyway. Travis had confronted this kind of thing many times when he'd been on the police force: a witness or neighbor just hadn't wanted to get involved with a police investigation, so they claimed not to have been home or seen anything. It wasn't uncommon, unfortunately.

Travis left a message for Jace, asking him to call, and then suggested to Chelsea that their best course of action would be to give Jace a little time to get back to them. Keeping things cordial went a long way toward getting people to help when you were a private investigator, he explained.

He could tell Chelsea didn't like it, but there was nothing more they could do about Jace right then.

Hoping to get some good news, he suggested they stop by the police station and see if Owens had made any progress finding out who had vandalized Chelsea's house. Travis didn't relish walking into the station, so he called Owens on his cell and arranged to meet the detective in a small park near the station's parking lot.

When they arrived, Travis parked in one of the visitor spaces. It had been almost four years since he'd left the force; been forced to leave, really, since he could no longer trust that his colleagues would have his back when bad stuff happened. Still, he felt a little tug in his chest looking up at the building that had been his professional home at one point.

They got out and made their way to the lone picnic table on the small patch of land next to the parking lot.

"Where is he? I don't see him," Chelsea said, shading her eyes from the glaring sun and scanning the short expanse between the station and where they stood.

Travis checked his phone to make sure he hadn't missed a message from Owens. He hadn't. "He probably just got caught up in something. He'll be here."

"Well, well. I thought I smelled something foul."

Travis stiffened, instantly on alert. He turned and found Detective Robert Ward. Ward had a wrapped sandwich in one hand and a to-go cup in the other. They were from the deli two blocks over that was a frequent cop stop for lunch. Travis missed their pastrami on rye, but he hadn't dared patronize the place since he had resigned from the force.

Ward swaggered toward them, a glower on his face. He cut a glance at Chelsea, dismissing her quickly, for which Travis gave small thanks. Ward hadn't worked on Franklin Brooks's case, so he likely didn't recognize Chelsea.

Ward could have been out of Central Casting playing

the stereotypical not-so-bright middle-aged cop. His shirt strained against his belly, and his sport coat was several years out of fashion.

Travis folded his arms over his chest and angled himself so he was slightly in front of Chelsea. "Ward," he greeted the man without a hint of warmth in his tone.

"What are you doing here, Collins? I hope not looking to get your job back," Ward sneered.

"I've got a job."

Ward snapped his fingers theatrically, as though he'd forgotten. The sound was like the crack of a whip in the otherwise quiet park. "That's right. You're a PI now," he said. "That's a club that doesn't mind a Judas is in their midst."

"Who is this jerk?" Chelsea said from behind Travis. Her voice was low enough that he didn't think Ward heard. Or maybe Ward was just so focused on his hatred for him that he couldn't be bothered to respond to Chelsea's slight.

Either way, Travis gave his head a slight shake and nudged Chelsea a little farther behind him. He didn't think Ward would lash out physically, but the man's disdain for Travis was clear. Who knew how worked up he would get himself?

"Every one of the cops I turned into internal affairs was either fired or forced to resign from the force," Travis responded.

"Internal affairs pigs covering their behinds," Ward spat. "That doesn't mean anything. I knew those men. They were good cops."

"They were supposed to uphold the law, not break it." Travis knew he was talking to a brick wall. Ward was not the kind of cop who would ever see it his way.

"Don't give me that crap. We do what we have to do to get the bad guys off the street."

"Not when it means becoming the bad guy."

"Who decides who's a good guy and who's a bad guy? You?" Ward scoffed.

"Well, it sure as hell shouldn't be you," Travis shot back.

Ward's face reddened. But before he could mount a comeback, Owens jogged over.

"Ward, the lieutenant is looking for you."

Ward cut a glance at Owens, but Owens kept his expression impassive. Ward shot one last venomous look at Travis before stomping away.

"I'm sorry if you're going to catch flak for meeting with me," Travis said to Owens when Ward was out of earshot.

Owens waived his apology away. "Don't worry about it. The vandalism at Chelsea's house is my case. Officially, I'm meeting with her. If she wants to bring you along..." He shrugged. "Who am I to argue?"

Owens was a good man and a good cop.

"So do you have anything for us?" Chelsea asked, getting the meeting on track.

"I wish I had better news," Owens answered. "Your ex-husband has an alibi for the vandalism. He was in surgery all day. Confirmed by multiple people. The fingerprints turned up nothing. They were all yours, Travis's or too smudged to be of any value. Whoever broke in probably wore gloves. I've turned up no witnesses. Not surprising since most of your neighbors were at work. I'm sorry, Ms. Harper."

"Please, call me Chelsea."

Nothing but dead ends, Travis thought, frustrated.

"I have to get back inside, but listen..." Owens stole a glance over his shoulder at the station before turning back to Travis and Chelsea. "I have a bad feeling about whatever you two have gotten yourself into."

"Are we still talking about the vandalism or Chelsea investigating her father's case?" Travis asked.

"Both. As you well know, they are probably one and the same. That's part of why I have a bad feeling. All I'm trying to say is be careful."

All three of them looked at the police station now. Ward had disappeared inside, and Travis had no doubt several of his former colleagues were at that very moment discovering he was currently nearby.

"There are a lot of people who would like to see you go down," Owens said in all seriousness. "By any means necessary."

Chapter Eighteen

Chelsea and Travis stopped by the hardware store and picked up cleaning supplies and paint and primer to cover the mess the vandal had left on her living room walls. When they got back to her house, Chelsea started cleaning and getting the house back in order while Travis broke out the primer and got to work on the walls.

It was slow going, both painting and cleaning. Chelsea made note of items that weren't salvageable and would have to be replaced. Included in that list was pretty much every piece of paper she hadn't had in her binder. Thankfully, the most important stuff she'd scanned and saved to her computer. But printing everything out again would be another big job she'd need to tackle at some point.

She worked on her bedroom first, cleaning until she felt like she'd rubbed out the destructive presence of the stranger who had invaded her private space. She saved the clothing she could; the vandal had cut up several shirts and skirts and several of her bras and panties. The thought of a stranger handling her things made her stomach turn. She gathered the rest of her clothing into her laundry basket to be washed. Then she turned her attention to the other rooms in the house.

The carpet in the living room had been splattered with paint along with the walls and would need to be taken up and replaced, but the kitchen and dining room floors got a thorough mopping. She cleaned until her hip protested, then headed into the living room to see how Travis was faring.

Red paint wasn't easy to cover, and the vandal had splattered all four of her living room walls. Travis had finally gotten enough primer on the walls to cover them, but there was no time to move on to painting.

Chelsea packed a few more clothes, including her favorite little black dress and the strappy heels she'd bought months earlier even though she'd had nowhere to wear them then. She had somewhere to wear them now. Contrary to her frequent reminders that this wasn't a date. They were working together to clear her father, and that was what she had to keep her focus on. But it definitely felt like a date when Travis picked her up in his living room at 8:00 p.m. sharp as they'd agreed. Wearing black dress pants and a button-down blue shirt that hugged his chest under a dark sport coat, he looked…delicious.

She was glad she'd opted for her little black dress when they stepped into the Fireside Grill, one of Los Angeles' nicest steak houses.

"This is a nice place," Chelsea said.

Travis's brow quirked up. "You didn't think I was going to take you to a nice place?"

"I…I didn't mean to imply—"

"I was joking. You made me a gourmet meal. I'm returning the favor." He turned to the hostess and gave his name for the reservation.

Chelsea wasn't sure if her ragù would qualify as gourmet, but she wasn't going to turn down dinner at the Fireside Grill, either.

The hostess led them to a table in an intimate corner

of the restaurant. She handed them each a menu and left them with a promise that their server would be with them soon. Chelsea's stomach flip-flopped. *Not a date*, she reminded herself.

The restaurant was fairly busy. This was probably just one of the only tables available. Still, she couldn't help but feel a little nervous energy. She could tell herself it wasn't a date all she wanted, but she hadn't been out with a man in longer than she was willing to admit, and her body seemed anxious to make up for lost time.

The flickering candle at the center of the table cast a shadow on Travis's face that made him appear even more ruggedly handsome than he already was. Leagues sexier actually. For a brief moment, she wondered what he would do if she rounded the table, sat on his lap and kissed him silly.

"Chelsea?" His voice pulled her from her fantasy.

She shook herself out of her racing thoughts and focused on the present. "Sorry, yes?"

A small, knowing smile crossed Travis's face. "Where did you go?"

"I was just thinking about the menu," she said, heat crawling up her neck. There was no doubt he knew she was lying. The menu was still closed in her hand. She opened it and hid behind it. She spent the next several minutes choosing her appetizer and entrée and reining in her libido.

The waitress stopped by their table and they put in their drink order. They continued to make small talk until the drinks arrived and then ordered their appetizers and entrées.

"So, um, do you have any siblings?" Chelsea asked, taking a swig from her glass of wine.

Travis's lips quirked up. "Do I have any siblings?"

"Give me a break," Chelsea laughed. "This is awkward. I'm trying to make conversation."

Travis chuckled, the low rumble sending a tingle down her back. "Okay. I'll lay off." His smile dimmed. "I had an older brother. He died when I was ten. He was thirteen." Travis lifted his wineglass to his lips.

"Oh, I'm sorry," she said, kicking herself. "I didn't know."

"Of course you didn't. It's fine." He laid his index finger over the rim of his glass. "I don't mind talking about him. Charles, his name was Charles. He was a cool kid. At least I thought so. As far as I was concerned, he hung the moon." He smiled again.

Chelsea laid her hand over his on the table. "How did he die, if you don't mind my asking?"

"It was a car accident. He, my parents and I were in the car when we were hit by a drunk driver. Charles and my mom and dad didn't make it."

Her heart broke for him. "God, Travis. I'm so sorry."

He pressed his lips tightly together. "Thanks. I spent the next eight years in foster care. Twelve homes in eight years to be exact. I think it's why I went into the marines. I craved structure after such an unstable childhood."

"And how long did you serve?"

He turned her hand over and traced the lines on her palm, sending a charge up and down her spine. "Eight years," he said with another chuckle. "A psychologist would probably have a field day with that coincidence."

"Was it just a coincidence?"

"Yes. Maybe. I don't know. After a while, I just felt like my time in the corps was up."

"And that's why you joined the LAPD?"

"Yeah." Now his laugh turned mirthless. "Not my best decision."

"I think it was a great decision." She took another sip of wine. She needed to be careful. She wasn't a big drinker. Not much of one at all really. She didn't want to make a fool of herself tonight. "You brought corruption to light."

"Yeah, well, my former colleagues aren't as appreciative as you are."

"They should be. Dirty cops make the good ones look bad. They should want to out the bad ones, and if they don't, they should get into a different line of work. Preferably one that keeps them away from the public," she added passionately.

He grinned. "You sound like a real-life avenger. Or a member of the Justice League or something. A real-life superhero."

She dipped her head. "I'm no superhero. I just hate seeing injustice go uncorrected."

"I bet you're a superhero to your dad."

Before she could think of what to say to that, their food arrived. She had opted for the lamb while Travis had more traditional fare for a steak house and ordered steak. They both had veggies on the side, and the waitress refilled their wineglasses before leaving again.

Chelsea took a bite of her food and moaned slightly as the spicy flavors mingled with the lamb hit her tongue. "This is amazing," she said around the food.

"I'm glad you like it," Travis said, his eyes sparkling. He cut into his steak. "A buddy of mine is the executive chef here. That's how I was able to get a reservation at the last moment. I was hoping to introduce you, but he's out of town."

"Well, your buddy sure knows what he's doing. You should get him to teach you."

"I think I'll stick to omelets and pancakes." Travis popped a piece of steak into his mouth, and they spent the next few minutes eating in companionable silence.

"I told you something about me," he said at last. "It's your turn to tell me something about you."

Chelsea leaned back a bit, surprised by his question. He hadn't shown much interest at all in her life outside of looking into her father's case. But she had asked him questions about his personal life. It was only fair that she answered his questions about hers. "You already know more about me than most people."

"I know about your father's case," he said pointedly. "I want to know about you, Chelsea."

She took another sip of wine, shifting in her seat. "What do you want to know?"

"Anything. Did you always want to be a teacher?"

She put her glass down and picked up her fork again but didn't bring it to her mouth. "No. I wanted to be an attorney, if you can believe it."

Travis pointed at her. "Now that I can believe. Why didn't you go to law school?"

She shrugged. "Money. After my dad was convicted, I needed to get a job quickly if I wanted to help pay for the appeals. I found a position with a small private school in San Francisco and got my master's degree at night. Then I switched to the public school system and moved back here to be closer to Aunt Brenda and Victor. And my dad. Don't get me wrong, I love my kids—"

"But you still think about law?"

"Sometimes. I mean, it's hard not to consider it. I almost feel like I don't need law school now. I have practically lived the law for the past several years."

"It couldn't have been easy."

"It wasn't. When I got word that Dad lost his last appeal..." She let the thought hang, mostly because she couldn't adequately put into words the desolation she had felt. She guessed this was how he felt talking about his family. Time to get this dinner conversation back on track. "What do you like to do for fun?" she asked, spearing another piece of lamb.

"Fun?"

"Yes," she said with a laugh. "You know, enjoyment. To bring pleasure to your life."

He leaned forward, the candlelight sparkling in his eyes along with a hint of something sensual. "Believe me, I enjoy pleasure, and I know many ways to have fun." His gaze raked over her face.

A part of her wanted to look away, but a bigger part wanted to lean into the suggestion he was making. She felt ready to burst into flames under his gaze.

"How are you two doing over here? Can I get you anything else?" the waitress singsonged, oblivious to the moment she had interrupted.

"We're great, thanks." Travis leaned back in his chair, but his gaze didn't move from Chelsea's face. "We'd like to see the dessert menu, please."

"Certainly," the waitress said, sailing off to get the menus.

"I probably shouldn't."

"Come on now, weren't you the one who just mentioned fun? Where's the fun in skipping dessert?"

Were her eyes deceiving her or had he licked his lips

after the word *dessert*? She was really on the edge of bursting into flames. Any minute now.

The waitress brought over dessert menus, and Chelsea scanned hers, thinking about the unexpected turn the night had taken. When Travis suggested dinner, she figured it was a pity thing. *Poor Chelsea who hasn't been out on a date in forever.* But she was not only enjoying spending time with him and getting to know him a little better, she enjoyed his flirting. *Wait.* Was that a pity thing, too? Was he throwing her a bone?

She glanced at him over the top of the menu. Even if he was, so what? This non-date couldn't mean anything anyway. It was nice getting to know him, and the flirting was a much-needed ego boost. She felt that she understood him a little better and trusted him a little more, but that was all this could lead to.

When the waitress returned, Chelsea ordered the chocolate mousse and he got the seven-layer cake. They both ordered coffee. They chatted more about their lives until the dessert arrived.

This time it was Travis who moaned when he tasted the cake. She was glad she was sitting when he did. Her knees wouldn't have held her up.

Travis placed a bite of cake onto his fork and leaned across the table with it outstretched toward her. "Try it."

Hunger for a very different kind of dessert seared through her.

"You like it?" he asked.

Her first attempt at answering failed. She leaned back in her seat and cleared her throat before trying again. "It's good," she said. "Great, really."

They finished their desserts quickly, and Travis paid

the check. They picked up their coats from the coat check and stepped out into the night.

"Thank you for a wonderful evening," Chelsea said.

"You're welcome." Travis shot her a heated gaze.

The valet rushed toward them, and Travis handed over his ticket.

The brisk wind sent a shiver through Chelsea. Travis put his arm around her, pulling her into his side. "Is this all right? Better?"

The spicy scent of his cologne snaked under her nose. "It's fine. Thanks." She looked up at him and found his face only centimeters away from hers.

Travis sucked in a breath and leaned closer. His lips slowly lowered until they were covering hers. She sighed, opening farther and letting him pull her in closer. The kiss was gentle but hot in a way she'd never experienced before. His hips pressed against her, and she felt the length of him. How much he wanted her. As much as she wanted him.

The kiss went on and on but not long enough. A boisterous group turned the corner, laughing loudly and heading to the restaurant.

Chelsea pulled away, her entire body still ignited from Travis's kiss. A kiss that had been everything she'd imagined and more, but the doubts and second thoughts were already creeping in. She needed him to get her father out of prison. That was the most important thing to her. Even if being in his arms made her forget about all the obstacles she was facing. But she could not mess that up. No matter how strong her feelings for Travis were growing.

She took one step back and then another, putting distance between them. She watched disappointment flit across Travis's face. Disappointment she knew was mirrored in her own expression. But this was for the best.

The valet pulled Travis's car to a stop at the curb in front of them and got out.

Travis turned to the young man.

A loud bang split the air, and Chelsea dropped to the pavement.

Chapter Nineteen

Chelsea jerked to one side, then fell to the sidewalk. In two steps, Travis was by her side, shielding her with his body. Tires squealed, and people were yelling around him, but all he could see was Chelsea's teary eyes staring up at him, her face contorted with pain. Blood poured from her arm, her sleeveless dress giving him a good view of the wound.

"I've got you. I've got you, Chelsea." He stripped off his jacket and button-down shirt and used the latter to press on the wound. She moaned.

"It's okay," he said. "You are going to be okay."

"Oh, man. Oh, my God. He shot her," the valet said in a high-pitched voice filled with panic.

"Call 911. Tell them we need an ambulance and that we have a gunshot wound. And tell the dispatcher that the victim is Chelsea Harper. Ask them to notify Owens," Travis barked out orders.

"Yes, sir. Got it." The valet dashed away.

"It hurts," Chelsea moaned.

"I know, baby. Hang in there. Help is on the way."

How had things gone bad so fast? He'd let down his guard. Been distracted. He'd let his attraction to Chelsea cloud his judgment, and she'd paid the price. If she died... He shook the thought away. She wasn't going to die. He pressed harder on the wound in an attempt to slow the bleeding.

The sound of sirens cut through the air, letting him know that the EMTs were close. Moments later they arrived, a man and a woman in blue. They pushed him to the side so they could kneel next to Chelsea. He stayed close, though, not wanting to let her out of his sight.

She must have felt the same way. Her eyes didn't leave his face even as the EMTs worked on her.

"Sir?"

Travis snapped his head to the right. A uniformed police officer stood next to him.

"Could you step over here and give me your statement of what happened?" the officer said.

"I'm not leaving her," Travis snarled.

The officer frowned. "Sir, I need to get your statement."

Travis gave the officer a succinct version of the moments leading up to Chelsea getting shot without moving away from her side.

"Let's get loaded up," the male EMT said. He and his partner lifted Chelsea onto a gurney and began pushing her toward the ambulance. Travis moved to follow.

"Hey!" The officer he'd been talking to put a hand on his forearm to stop him. "You need to stay here and finish giving me your statement."

Travis shook off the officer's hand. "I am not leaving her," he repeated.

"It's okay, Officer."

Travis and the officer turned as Owens stopped next to them. "I can get his formal statement at the hospital."

The officer scowled at Owen's badge but stepped back.

Travis jogged to catch up with the gurney, and Owens hustled to keep up.

"What happened?" Owens asked.

"Drive-by. I didn't see the driver. Black sedan. I can't tell you anything about the plates. They were covered. Just like with the hit-and-run video, although this was a different car." Travis pulled himself into the back of the ambulance.

"I'll meet you at the hospital," Owens said.

Travis turned and shot Owens a look that had made lesser men tremble with fear. "Owens, when we find this guy, I want to be the one to take him down. Understand?"

TRAVIS WATCHED THE doctor examine Chelsea from the corner of the room where he'd been since the EMTs had rolled her into the hospital on a gurney. Watching over her like he should have been doing before she was shot. He was still kicking himself for letting his growing feelings for her sway his professionalism. Chelsea's injury might not be lethal, but it was painful. He could see that from the semi-glazed look in her eyes.

"Travis? Are you still there?" Kevin's voice cut through Travis's thoughts.

"Yeah, I'm still here," he said into the phone.

"Are you sure you're okay? I can come down to the hospital."

"No, I'm fine. Chelsea's going to be okay, too." The bullet had only grazed her arm, thankfully.

"Good. Then you should know that I was able to get an address for Peter Schmeichel. He does still live in Monterey. I found his name and a photograph in a church bulletin. Looks like he volunteers a lot of his time."

"Send me everything you got." Travis glanced at Chelsea again. "I'm not sure when I'll be able to make a trip to Monterey." The picturesque town was nearly a six-hour drive away. "But I have a buddy who owns a condo there. I'll give him a call. See if I can crash there for a night or two in the coming days."

"If you need me or Tess to head up there for you…"

Travis looked at Chelsea again. He didn't want to leave her side, but he knew this investigation better than Tess or Kevin, and he wanted to see how Peter would respond to his questions. "No. I'll go." He ended the call with Kevin.

Seconds later, his phone pinged with a text containing Peter's address and the church bulletin Kevin mentioned. Travis shot off a quick text to his friend asking if his Monterey condo was available for the next several days and whether he could crash there, then walked over to the bed where Chelsea lay.

"You are very lucky," the doctor said as she finished the last of Chelsea's stitches. Dr. Lacey's curly brown hair was bound on top of her head with a hair tie, and wrinkles creased her forehead. Intelligent eyes indicated that she knew what she was doing. She pulled off her gloves and tossed them onto a metal table next to Chelsea. "I'll prescribe a painkiller, but you'll be able to sleep in your own bed tonight."

Chelsea cut a look at Travis. "Not exactly, but thanks, Doctor."

Dr. Lacey made notes on a tablet. "It may take me a little while to get your discharge papers together. Just hang tight. We're a bit understaffed tonight."

"As long as I don't have to stay overnight, I'll be fine," Chelsea responded.

"You shouldn't be so eager to leave," Travis said after

the doctor left the room. "At least we know you're safe in the hospital."

Chelsea tilted her head and looked at him. "I'm safe at your place, too."

"I'm not so sure about that anymore," he muttered, running a hand over his head.

Chelsea studied him. "What does that mean?"

"It means I'm the reason you got shot."

Chelsea frowned. "Did you hit your head?"

"Chels, I'm serious."

"So am I. Did you hit your head when you threw your body over me? Because admittedly things happened fast, but I don't recall you shooting at me."

"I was distracted. I should have been paying attention. I should have seen the sedan and the gun before the shooter got off a shot. If I had been doing my job—"

"Wait a minute." She held up a hand. "I hired you to help me prove my father's innocence, not throw yourself in front of bullets for me."

"I know, but of the two of us, I'm the professional."

Chelsea pushed herself up straighter in the hospital bed. "Oh, get over yourself. You are no more responsible for me getting shot then I am. You're not a superhero. If you had seen the guy and thrown yourself in front of me, you would have been shot. Would you be saying the same things to me right now if our roles were reversed?"

"I'd tell you that you weren't to blame," he reluctantly admitted.

"Okay, then, I don't want to hear any more of this macho 'I should have protected you' baloney."

Despite everything, he smiled.

A moment later, that smile fell as Chelsea's aunt Brenda barreled through the door.

"There you are. Oh, my God, Chelsea." Her aunt threw herself on top of Chelsea, her sobs filling the room.

Chelsea flinched with pain from her aunt's jostling.

Travis took a step toward them, intending to prod the older woman away before she inadvertently hurt her niece any further. But the man from the photo on Chelsea's dresser, her cousin Victor, strode in after Brenda.

Victor sized Travis up quickly. "You must be the private investigator my mom told me was helping Chels."

Travis nodded, bracing himself for the same anger Chelsea's aunt had thrown his way at her house.

Victor thrust his hand out. "Victor Harper, Chelsea's cousin. More like a brother. Thanks for looking out for my cuz."

Travis shook Victor's hand, surprised by the friendly greeting.

"Chelsea told us how you used your own body to shield her and that you tried to stop the bleeding," Victor explained.

Chelsea had called her family herself after the doctor determined her wound wouldn't require surgery and they'd been waiting for her to get stitched up. She'd wanted privacy for the call, so Travis had stepped into the hall while she was on the phone. Apparently, she had embellished his role.

"I really didn't do that much," he countered to Victor.

"Yes, he did," Chelsea called from the bed.

Chelsea's aunt lifted herself from Chelsea's body and made a half turn. "You," she said, stalking across the room to Travis.

Victor moved quickly, getting out of the path of his mother.

Before Travis knew what she was about to do, Aunt

Brenda had her arms wrapped around him. She buried her face in his chest, still crying.

"Thank you," she said, her voice thick with emotion. "You saved my Chelsea."

Travis rubbed her shoulder awkwardly. "You're welcome, but really I—"

Aunt Brenda reared back, fire mingling with the tears in her eyes. "Don't say it was nothing. It was everything to me. To Victor. Chelsea is family. She told me you ruined a beautiful shirt, and you stayed with her when she was scared. That's not nothing."

"She would have done the same for me," he said, still unsure what to do with the older woman's praise.

"That is true," Aunt Brenda said. "My Chelsea has a big heart." She patted one of Travis's cheeks. "So do you. I can tell."

"Thank you," Travis said, touched by her words.

"I was rude to you the other day when you came to my house. Let me make it up to you? You have to come to dinner. Do you like mashed potatoes and gravy? I make them with real potatoes. None of that powdered junk. Milk and real butter, that's the secret to getting them nice and fluffy." She patted his cheek again.

Victor edged up to his mother. "Okay, Ma. I think now is not a good time to try to feed the man." He wrapped an arm around his mother, but she shrugged him off.

"It's always a good time to feed a man." Brenda turned back to look at her niece. "You hear that, Chelsea?" She winked at her.

"Aunt Brenda," Chelsea groaned.

"Ma," Victor lamented.

Travis held back a chuckle, but he was struck by a sense of longing. He never let himself think about what might have been if his family had lived, but occasionally a memory would creep up on him. They had been a happy family. Content to be in each other's company. His brother had teased him sometimes, and it had annoyed him then, but Travis would give anything to have his brother tease him again. Or fight with him. Having people in his life who cared enough to fight with him and for him… It had been a long time since he had that. Maybe too long.

He told himself he didn't need it, but watching Chelsea with her aunt and her cousin, who had raced to the hospital the minute they learned she was hurt, made him realize he'd been lying to himself. He wanted people in his life, that sense of belonging to a family. Maybe even this family.

He watched Chelsea's aunt and cousin fuss over her while foggy images of what his future could look like played through his head. What if he let Chelsea in?

The door to the room swung open, and Dr. Lacey strode back in. "Well, it looks like the gang's all here. I'm going to have to ask you to step into the hall while I talk to Miss Harper about caring for her wound. When we're done, she will be all set to go home."

Victor ushered his mother out into the hall.

Travis started to follow but stopped at the sound of Chelsea's voice.

"Hey, are you okay?" she asked him.

Was he? He wasn't sure. He felt like a raw nerve at the moment. But he wasn't going to trouble Chelsea with his kaleidoscope of emotions. Especially not when he wasn't sure what to make of them himself.

Instead, he smiled. "I'm fine. Great, now that we know you're going to be okay."

"Okay," she said, a note of skepticism in her voice.

"I'll be waiting for you when you're ready to go home."

Chapter Twenty

Travis helped Chelsea into his guest room, then left her to change into her pajamas. It had been a long and arduous night, and she was exhausted. And despite knowing she was safe now, a thread of fear still lingered. She could hear Travis walking around the house, checking all the locks on the doors and windows, she suspected.

She'd changed and was crossing from the attached bathroom to the bed when he appeared at the bedroom door again.

"Here. Let me help you." He put an arm around her shoulders, walked her to the head of the bed and turned down the bedspread with one hand.

"You know, I'm not an invalid. I can walk."

He eased her down onto the bed. "I know you aren't, but you should take it easy for a while. And speaking of taking it easy, Kevin found an address for Peter Schmeichel. It's in Monterey, so I was thinking I could have Kevin or Tess stay with you while I go speak to him."

Chelsea swung her legs up onto the bed and under the bedspread. "Without me? No way." She shook her head. "I'm going with you."

He sighed. "I had a feeling you'd say that. We'll go in a few days then. Once you've had some time to rest."

"I don't need rest, and I don't want to put off talking to Peter. We can go tomorrow."

Travis pulled the covers up to her waist. "You were just shot."

She tamped down the fear that threatened to rise. "It was a graze."

He rolled his eyes. "Semantics."

Chelsea grabbed his hand. "Travis, please. We're close. I can feel it. I don't want to wait. I need to do this."

He sighed again. "Okay. As long as you're feeling up for it tomorrow, we can go. But if you don't feel like it when you wake up tomorrow, you have to promise you'll tell me." He looked into her eyes, and she saw how serious he was. "I won't compromise your health."

Warmth spread through her chest. She squeezed his hand. "I appreciate you looking out for me." She threw good sense to the wind and leaned forward and kissed his mouth quickly, softly.

He stroked her cheek with the pad of his thumb. "Get some sleep." He stood and headed for the door.

"Travis?" Her heart pounded in her chest. She felt a little foolish, but fear pushed her forward.

Travis turned.

"Would you mind staying with me tonight? Just sleeping. I'm embarrassed to admit it, but I'm still a little shaky after, well, everything."

"You have nothing to be embarrassed about," he said, heading back to the bed.

She scooted over to make room for him. He toed off his shoes and slid in beside her still in his clothes. She relaxed against him. He wrapped an arm around her waist and gathered her close. The faint smell of his cologne still lingered even after the night they'd had.

"I feel safe when I'm with you."

"I'm glad I make you feel safe."

His breath tickled the skin on her neck, causing her pulse to pick up. She'd meant it when she asked him to only sleep next to her, but her body didn't seem to want to cooperate. Lying next to him was sweet torture but still torture. "You do," she said.

"You know, when I woke up in the hospital and the doctor told me that my parents and brother had been killed, that was the most scared I thought I could ever be. Until today. I've never been more scared than I was when I saw you lying on the pavement with a gunshot wound."

"I'm sorry I scared you like that."

He shifted so he could look at her. "You don't have anything to be sorry about. I'm just so glad you're safe." He held her more tightly against his side.

She snaked a hand up around the back of his neck and leaned forward. As soon as their lips met, his control seemed to snap. He ravished her mouth, sending a groan through them both. Blood pounded in her ears. She deepened the kiss, letting her hand move down from his neck to his chest before venturing farther south. He stopped her before she reached below his waist.

"Wait. Chelsea. I…" He panted. "I think we should slow down. This… We… I'm not a relationship guy," he blurted.

She stiffened.

"I mean… I didn't mean. I just wanted to be upfront about—"

"I get it." She slid away from him.

"I'm not trying to hurt you. Obviously, I'm attracted to you, but you deserve a man who is going to be all in, and I'm not that guy."

"I said I get it, Travis," she said, her tone more caustic than she'd intended. She couldn't be mad with him for saying out loud exactly what she'd been telling herself for days now. She let out a breath. "You're right." She laid her head on his shoulder. "You'll stay until I fall asleep?"

"Of course. Whatever you want."

When she woke the next morning, the side of the bed where he'd been was cold.

TRAVIS WAS UP at six the next morning. He normally went to the gym, but he wasn't about to leave Chelsea's side, so he settled for a pared-down workout in his bedroom. The drive to Monterey took about five hours, and he wanted to arrive by early afternoon, but he was loath to wake Chelsea. She needed rest to heal. Part of him hoped she would sleep late so he'd have a reason to put off the trip for another day and give her more time to rest, but he should have known it wouldn't be that easy. He heard her moving around the guest room shortly after 7:30.

He still had a knot in his throat thinking about their conversation the night before.

You did the right thing.

He knew he had. Chelsea deserved the truth from him. He wasn't the type of man who did relationships, no matter how brilliant, sexy and fearless the woman. And Chelsea was all of those things. She deserved someone who could commit to her. That wasn't him.

He'd just finished cooking the first batch of waffles when Chelsea entered the kitchen. She looked much better than she had the night before. The color was back in her cheeks, and she appeared rested. But her body language was closed off. She gave him a weak, polite smile as she headed for the coffee maker. "Good morning."

"Good morning. I hope you like waffles," he said.

"I do."

"How many?"

"Two, please."

He handed her a plate with a couple waffles he'd just taken off the iron.

She took it without meeting his gaze. "Thanks."

He had never done the awkward morning-after dance before. He rarely stayed the night. He blew out a silent breath and put two more waffles on the griddle for himself. When they were ready, he sat across from Chelsea. They ate in uncomfortable silence for several minutes.

"Are you still up for the trip to Monterey?"

"Absolutely." Chelsea dabbed her mouth with a napkin and rose. "I just need to pack a few more things. When do you want to leave?"

The clock on the stove read 8:15 a.m. "Does nine o'clock work for you? We should get there around three if we don't make a lot of stops and don't hit traffic. Peter works the three-to-eleven shift at a plumbing supply distributor, so that will give us a little time to settle in at the condo before going to see him."

"That's fine. I'll go get ready." She all but ran from the kitchen.

He sighed. There wasn't anything he could do about the awkwardness except hope it passed. He cleaned up the kitchen before gathering his own overnight bag. Chelsea met him at the car at nine o'clock sharp, and they headed out.

He headed north on US 101 toward Santa Barbara. It would be marginally faster to take the I-5 north, but the 101 ran along the coast and provided a much better view. They kept the conversation light and mostly talked about the case. As he hoped, some of the awkwardness from the night before ebbed the farther they got from his house.

Chelsea fell asleep somewhere around Pismo Beach. He shut off the radio to let her sleep, content to make the drive in silence. He couldn't help but note how he seemed to be content to do just about anything when he was with her.

She woke as he exited the freeway and drove into what was known as Old Monterey just before 3:00 p.m. They drove past a gallery, specialty markets, several restaurants, pubs and coffee shops. Everything about the area screamed small-town America.

"Do you like seafood?" he asked her, turning the car away from the downtown area.

"Yeah. I love it," she said, stretching.

"Great. I need to make a stop before we get to the condo."

Travis drove a few miles before he pulled into a parking lot twenty-five yards from the wharf.

"Where are we?"

"This is my favorite place to buy seafood." He opened his door.

Chelsea pushed open her door and followed Travis into what looked like an aluminum shack. Inside there were several rows of tables with seafood displayed on ice. Running along the far wall was a counter with more fish behind glass.

The muscular young man behind the counter greeted them. "What can I get you folks?"

"Two lobsters, a pound of shrimp and a half pound of crab."

While the clerk pulled his order together, Travis walked around the shop collecting the other items he'd need to prepare lunch, as well as a six pack of beer.

"This seems like a lot," Chelsea said, following him.

"Trust me," he said.

They went back to the counter and gathered their order. "Anything else I can get you?" the man asked.

"That should do it," Travis said.

The clerk put everything into bags and rang them up. Travis paid, and they got back into the car and headed a little farther up the coast until they reached a strip of beachfront condos. He pulled the car into a short, shared driveway. The ocean was visible just beyond the side of the house, the water a brilliant calm blue past a smooth expanse of sand.

Travis had spent many weekends decompressing here. His friend actually owned a couple condos as investment properties, but it looked like the left side of the house was empty at the moment. Inside, the condo was renovated and well maintained. Two good-size bedrooms opened up off the large living/dining/kitchen area. A wide balcony jutted off the back of the condo, looking out into the ocean.

"Take whichever room you'd like," Travis said, placing the grocery bag on the counter. He grabbed the lobsters and put them in the fridge.

Chelsea carried her bag into the room on the left. It was slightly bigger and had a better view in his opinion. It was the room he usually slept in, but he was happy to give it up to her.

He opened one of the beers and put the others in the fridge. Then he grabbed a large pot from a lower cabinet and filled it with water, setting it on a burner to boil. Next, he got started preparing the easy crab dip recipe he always used, then arranged some crackers on a plate and scooped cocktail sauce into a small bowl. When the water came to a boil, he pulled the lobsters from the fridge. The cool air had done its job putting the crustaceans to sleep. Cooking them this way seemed less cruel than throwing them into boiling water while they were still active.

He was spreading the shrimp out on a platter next to the cocktail sauce when Chelsea stepped out of her bedroom.

"This is a gorgeous place. And these photos," she said, stopping next to a nighttime photo of the ocean just beyond her bedroom door.

Travis poured her a glass of wine. "My buddy who owns the condo is a photographer."

"He's really good." Chelsea crossed to the kitchen and took the glass of wine from him.

He smiled. "He's Myles Messina."

Chelsea's hand froze with her glass halfway to her lips. "Myles Messina, the famous photographer?"

Travis nodded.

"Wow. How do you two know each other?"

"Myles was in foster care with me for a year. We managed to keep in touch after we aged out of the system."

"I didn't know he was in foster care." Chelsea sat on one of the kitchen counter stools.

"Yeah, he's a real success story."

"Both of you are." Chelsea brought the wineglass to her lips.

Heat traveled through him at the compliment. He lifted the plates with the shrimp and crab dip and carried them to the balcony door. "Can you open this for me?"

Chelsea grabbed the door handle and turned it. They stepped out onto the deck. A glass-top table with four wrought iron chairs stood center stage.

"Don't sit yet." Travis set the food on the table, then went back into the house. He returned moments later with two towels and his beer.

They both sat. Travis took a deep breath of ocean air, feeling it calm him. There was something special about the beach air here. Cleaner. He took another sip of beer and watched Chelsea reach for a shrimp and dip it into the sauce.

"Oh," she moaned, sending a spirit of need to his lower region. "This is amazing."

"Yeah, the crab house makes the best cocktail sauce. Homemade by the owner," he said, trying not to think about how his body had reacted to her moan.

Her brows rose. "I thought you said you couldn't cook."

"You'll notice there's nothing that had to be seasoned or braised or anything much more difficult than dropping things into a pot of boiling water or mixing crab dip."

Chelsea laughed. "How often do you come here?"

"Recently, not as much as I'd like to. Work has been busy."

"Well, I can see why you like it." She leaned her head back against the chair and closed her eyes.

God, she was gorgeous.

They said in silence for a while until Chelsea said, "The lobster should be ready by now, shouldn't it?"

Travis got up. "You're right." Chelsea started to follow.

"No. You stay. Enjoy the view. I've got this."

He transferred the lobsters from the water onto a large platter and carried it outside with a dish of clarified garlic butter. He went back inside for the wine bottle and dinner plates.

"You know, I can get used to being served like this," Chelsea teased, grabbing a lobster and putting it on the plate he slid in front of her.

And I could get used to serving you. The thought popped into his head unbidden.

No. This was nice, but that's all it was. A nice moment. That's all it could be.

But even as he thought, he couldn't quite convince himself that was all this was.

"DO YOU NEED anything else?" Travis asked her, still standing next to the table.

"I don't think so. Sit. Relax," Chelsea said.

He sat down next to her. They ate in companionable silence until her phone rang. She pulled it from her pocket. Simon. She made a face and declined the call. The phone rang again a moment later.

"If you need to take that, you can," Travis said.

"No, it's just Simon." She declined the call again.

Travis's mouth twisted into a frown.

For some reason she felt she had to explain. "He's been calling me since I, we, threw him out of my house."

"Why?" Travis groaned.

"I don't know. I haven't taken his call."

Travis seemed relieved to hear her say that. She got the feeling he didn't want her taking Simon's call any more than she wanted to talk to her ex-husband.

Chelsea dipped a piece of lobster in butter. "This is the best butter I've ever tasted." She popped the lobster in her mouth. A little bit of butter dripped down her chin.

Travis reached out and swiped it away with his thumb.

The waves crashed against the sand, and electricity crackled between them.

Travis ran the pad of his thumb over her lips.

She knew she would probably kick herself later. He'd made it quite clear he was not available for anything serious, and she didn't do casual hookups. But she didn't care about any of that at the moment. She had to kiss him, the desire more than she had the will to fight off.

She leaned forward, closing the distance between them. Kissing him felt like a strong wave had crashed into her, dragging her underwater. His hands roamed over her shoulders, then down her back. He seemed to feel just as much urgency as she did.

Travis pulled back first. "We shouldn't do this." He slid his chair away from her.

"You're right," she said, turning away from him, her pride smarting. She was a glutton for punishment.

Travis rose. "I'm going to get us a couple of bottles of water." He went inside.

Water. He probably thought she'd had too much to drink. Maybe she had. He was right, she shouldn't have kissed him. No matter how good it felt. It was stupid.

Travis returned with the bottled waters, and she took the one he offered.

"How about a walk on the beach?" she suggested, mostly to get away from the scene of the kissing crime, as it were.

He agreed, and they set off along the beach, keeping a respectable distance between them. Travis told her a little bit more about his older brother, recounting several childhood stories. She reciprocated, telling him about growing up with Victor.

They'd made it about a mile down the beach when her phone began ringing again.

"Are you sure you don't want to take that?" Travis asked.

She silenced the ringer this time. "Absolutely sure."

"You know, I can't see the two of you together. How did you two meet?"

"Aunt Brenda took a fall four years ago. Simon was her orthopedist. I should have known better, but Dad's first appeal had just been denied, and I was in a tough place. We got married too quickly. Only five months after we met."

"That is fast."

"Too fast. We didn't really know each other at all. I think we were both infatuated with how different we were. Or maybe that was just me. I've learned that Simon always has ulterior motives."

"And what was his ulterior motive for marrying you?"

"I think he thought it would upset his father. Bringing a poor, Black girlfriend home. And to be truthful, I think his father was concerned at first."

"At first?"

"Funny enough, my former father-in-law and I had more in common than Simon and I did. Gerald passed away about six months ago."

"I'm sorry for your loss."

"Thanks. Gerald was a doctor like Simon, but he came from nothing. A poor boy from southern Texas. Worked his way through college and med school. He was brilliant and came up with a revolutionary procedure for conducting intestinal surgery. That made him a legend in the medical field and a millionaire many, many times over. I think Simon's issues stem from feeling like he can't live up to his father. I think Gerald thought that I might be good for Simon."

"But you weren't?"

Chelsea laughed. "Our marriage was a disaster. Before the first year was out, I realized I'd made a mistake. Simon was already stepping out with one of his coworkers. Our marriage didn't last much longer. I kept in touch with Gerald, though. He was a good man."

"He didn't have a problem with who your father was?"

She pushed a lock of hair from her face. Gerald had never bought up her father, at least not with her, but she was sure he'd cautioned Simon. "I'm sure he didn't love that his daughter-in-law had a convict for a father, but he was never anything but supportive."

"That's cool. He sounds like a good guy."

"He was. Can I ask you something?"

"Sure."

"You told me you don't do relationships." Her heart thudded uncontrollably. "Have you ever considered it? You know, doing a relationship."

Travis stopped walking and turned to look out at the ocean. He didn't answer her.

"I'm sorry. I shouldn't have asked." Chelsea said as her phone vibrated, indicating another incoming call.

"You should take that," Travis said, turning back to the condo. "I'm going to clean up. Peter should be getting a break soon."

She ignored her phone and watched him walk away.

Chapter Twenty-One

His nerves were on edge. Shooting at Chelsea had been a rash decision. Stupid. Especially since he hadn't killed her. The cops would have no choice but to investigate a shooting. They weren't the brightest bulbs in the pack, but even a dim bulb gave off some light. What if some upstart detective believed Chelsea's rants about her father's innocence?

He'd done it again. Let his emotions, his anger, take over. It was Chelsea's fault, just like it had been Lily's. They confused him. Forced him to take action when he just wanted to be left in peace. Lily had paid the price for angering him.

Blood roared in his ears. He could feel his life veering out of control again. Like it had when Lily was alive. He wasn't sure how to regain control, but he knew he had to. Chelsea Harper had to be dealt with. Once and for all.

Chapter Twenty-Two

Salinger's Wholesale Plumbing and Fixtures was located in an industrial park in Salinas about twenty miles from Monterey. Travis had called ahead and, using the bogus excuse of having talked to Peter earlier about some plumbing part, found out that Peter was scheduled to work that day from three to eleven that evening and that he usually took his dinner break around 7:00 p.m.

The manager of the warehouse pointed Peter out to Chelsea and Travis. Peter was pulling several large boxes on a dolly cart from one end of the warehouse to the other where the truck bays were. He wore a blue-gray jumpsuit unzipped enough for Travis to see the white T-shirt underneath. His name was stenciled on the jumpsuit's left side, and worn work boots covered his feet. He slowed and stopped as Travis and Chelsea approached.

"Peter," Travis said with a polite smile that he hoped would put the man at ease. "My name is Travis Collins. This is my associate Chelsea Harper. Can we speak with you for a moment?"

"About what?"

"Lily Wong," Chelsea answered.

Peter's body stiffened, going on full alert. "I don't have anything to say about that."

"I think you do, Peter," Travis said firmly. "Chelsea's aunt received an anonymous note saying you'd lied at trial. I think you sent it."

It was a shot in the dark, but from the way Peter paled, Travis knew he'd hit his mark. If Peter had sent the note, it meant he felt remorse for what he'd done. That was good for them.

"We have spoken to Gina." Travis paused for several beats, letting that statement percolate in Peter's head, leaving him wondering just what his ex-girlfriend had said about the night Lily was murdered. "We'll buy you dinner. Your manager said your break starts soon. Anywhere you want to go. Just give us ten minutes." Travis could see the man's resolve cracking. "Ten minutes, and you get a free dinner. How about it?"

"Ten minutes," Peter agreed. "There's a Thai place two blocks down. I'll meet you there in fifteen minutes."

"Thank you," Chelsea said before she and Travis turned and left the warehouse.

"You think he'll show?" she asked as they got into Travis's car and headed for the restaurant.

"I think so. If he doesn't, we'll track him down again and ask a lot less nicely."

Thankfully, they didn't have to. Peter arrived at the restaurant fifteen minutes later as promised. Their waiter had already left three waters and three menus on the table. Travis wasn't hungry, and apparently neither was Chelsea. They both had coffee. Peter went all in, getting stir-fry with soft-shell crab, the most expensive item on the menu. Travis only hoped the coming conversation would be worth what this dinner would cost.

When the waiter left to put their order in with the kitchen, Peter asked, "What do you want from me?"

"I don't know if you know, but Franklin Brooks is my father," Chelsea said.

Peter squinted at her from across the table. "I didn't recognize you. Yeah, yeah, I remember you now from the trial."

"My father has exhausted all his appeals. Barring the truth coming out, he's going to spend the rest of his life in jail."

Peter's gaze slid from Chelsea's. "I'm sorry to hear that."

"Are you?" Chelsea leaned forward. "Because I think you know my dad is innocent."

Peter wouldn't look at either of them. "I don't know anything."

"Mr. Schmeichel." Travis jumped back into the conversation. "We are trying to get an innocent man free from prison. We need your help."

Peter remained silent.

"My father's life is at stake. If you don't tell the truth now, he'll die in prison," Chelsea added.

Peter reached for his glass of water and took a long pull on the straw.

Chelsea and Travis waited.

Finally, Peter spoke. "The court said he's guilty."

"In part based on your testimony. But we all know that what you said on the witness stand wasn't true," Chelsea countered.

"Are you calling me a liar?"

"I think you may have seen a way out of a jam, and you took it," Travis said, avoiding the question.

"Oh, yeah? And you got all this figured out based on what?"

"Based on the fact that Franklin was somewhere else at the time you say he was at Lily's house. On the fact that Franklin has always professed his innocence. And on the fact that your recollection of seeing Franklin at Lily's house at the time of her murder is undermined by Gina's statement."

"Gina," Peter scoffed. "The cops didn't believe her."

"No, they didn't," Travis agreed. "But then they had an incentive not to believe her. A woman killed in her own home. The community was scared and demanding someone be arrested. The recent ex-boyfriend is an easy answer. They just needed enough evidence to slap the cuffs on him. But they had enough evidence to slap the cuffs on you."

Peter's angry gaze slipped away but not before Travis got a hint of the guilt there, too. He kept going. "You were arrested about a week after Lily's murder. Your third strike." Travis softened his tone. "No one could blame you for wanting to avoid prison. Did one of the detectives hint that they would be willing to make a deal if you had seen something helpful regarding Lily's murder?"

Travis half expected Peter to erupt with anger and denials, but neither came. Peter looked down at the table and sighed.

"You know how we found you?" Chelsea asked.

Peter looked up and shook his head.

"The church bulletin. Your name popped up as a parishioner of the month. You do a lot of good work at your church."

"I do," Peter confirmed.

The waiter returned with their food then. It took several moments to get settled, but when the waiter left again, Travis decided to push Peter a little harder. "You know, Chelsea and I don't think you were involved with Lily's murder. But I work with a team, and we bounce things off each other. It's been pointed out to me that you could have made up the story regarding Franklin not to get out of the drug charge, or at least not just to get out of the drug charge. That maybe you had another reason for wanting to throw suspicion on Franklin." Travis let the implication hang over the table.

"What are you suggesting?" Peter glared, ignoring his lunch.

"Well, and I'm just spitballing, but Lily was an attractive, professional, intelligent woman. A catch. And she was back on the market. We know she was dating again. And Gina mentioned you two were having trouble. Arguing a lot. Maybe you made a play for Lily. She said no, things got out of hand."

"No," Peter spat.

"Then what really happened?" Chelsea asked. "I know it wasn't what you testified to at my father's trial."

"You don't know anything."

"Oh, but we do." Travis said. "We know you lied. The cops may have dismissed Gina seven years ago, but we wouldn't let them get away with that now. And someone has been targeting Chelsea. Attempting to run her down, vandalizing her home, even shooting at her. That makes me very angry, Peter. It makes me think someone has something to hide. Maybe someone who has already lied under oath. Where were you yesterday between 8:00 and 11:00 p.m.?" Travis asked, giving the time period when Chelsea had been shot.

Peter pushed his chair back and started to stand. "I don't have to listen to this."

"Sit. Down."

Peter hesitated, half standing, half sitting for a fraction of a second before reclaiming his seat.

"Peter, my father has been in prison for seven years," Chelsea said in a soft voice. "You seem to have changed your life, turned over a new leaf. You're helping people now. Help my father. Right this wrong."

There was a long silence where no one at the table so much as moved beyond breathing.

Peter spoke first. "I have to admit I lied."

"You have to tell the truth," Chelsea responded.

"You sign an affidavit under oath saying that your testimony at Franklin Brooks's trial was inaccurate."

Peter laughed bitterly. "Inaccurate is just fancy talk for lied."

It was, so Travis stayed quiet.

"Everyone will know I'm a liar and I could get in real trouble."

"Everyone will know you're correcting a wrong," Chelsea countered. "Making amends for a mistake that you made. There's nothing shameful about that."

Peter's chin dropped to his chest. "I lied." His voice was so soft Travis wasn't sure he heard it. "I lied," Peter said, louder this time, and Travis nearly cheered.

Peter looked at Chelsea. "You said I've turned over a new leaf. Well, I've tried. I kicked the drugs. I started going to church. I got a decent job, but I've always felt guilty about what I did to your father. I don't know if he's innocent or not. The cop said he did it, and I didn't see any reason for both of us to go to jail back then, so I lied. But it was eating me alive that an innocent man might be sitting in prison in part because of me, so I sent the note to your aunt. I...I was too scared to go to the prosecutor myself, but I hoped that someone would look into it. Make sure a mistake hadn't been made."

Chelsea let out an audible breath.

Even Peter looked lighter. Like a weight had been lifted from his shoulders. He looked Chelsea in the eyes. "I'll sign your affidavit. I don't know how much it will help your father, but it's time I told the truth."

Chapter Twenty-Three

"I can't believe he admitted he lied," Chelsea said not for the first time since she and Travis had left Peter. They'd just walked into the condo, and she was euphoric. "I'm going to get my dad out of jail, Travis." She'd always believed that she'd do it someday, but someday finally felt like it was coming soon.

"Slow down," Travis said, probably attempting to temper her enthusiasm. But even he was grinning. "We still have a lot of work to do before we can go to the prosecutor."

But they were closer, and she had him to thank. Without thinking, she threw herself into his arms. "Thank you," she said, wrapping her arms around him and hugging him tightly. "You don't know what this means to me. What it means to me that you've helped."

His muscles flexed under her hands. "I will always be there for you, Chelsea. Whenever you need me."

The air between them was charged. She knew if she looked into his eyes now she'd see in them exactly what she was feeling. Want. Desire. Need. She leaned back, and there it was. She knew that there were a lot of good reasons they shouldn't do this, but she didn't care about any of them. She wanted Travis Collins, and from the look and feel of him, he wanted her, too.

She feathered a light kiss over his lips.

He sucked in a ragged breath. "What are you doing?"

She didn't answer right away. Instead, she kissed each corner of his mouth before dotting light kisses along his jawline. "What do you think I'm doing?"

"Chelsea—"

"Travis, I don't want to hear about all the reasons we shouldn't do this. I already know the reasons not to. I'm telling you that I want you. Do you want me?"

"You know I do, but—"

She pressed a finger to his lips. "No buts. No doubts. Just us, right now."

He growled, placing his palms on either side of her face and pulling her to him. His lips met hers in a kiss that was ruthlessly efficient. He lifted her. She wrapped her legs around his waist and let him carry her into his bedroom.

His chest rose and fell. She felt the beat of his heart and gazed up into his face. A heady desire coursed between them. Then his mouth met hers, kissing, nibbling, suckling. Somewhere in the heat of passion they both shed their clothes. Her lips were swollen with his skill. They were both breathless by the time he slid down her body, kissing her neck and shoulders before lavishing her breasts with attention.

He grabbed her wrists, pulling them both over her head, and rolled her flat onto her back. Then he came down over her, straddling her. He worked his way down her body, leaving a trail of kisses across her belly before making his way lower. She responded by opening herself to him, body and heart. His fingers explored her, and she sighed, giving in to the intimate caress and riding the wave of release when it came. The aftermath of her orgasm was still rippling through her when he came up over her again, having sheathed himself with a condom. Gently he coaxed her thighs open, his large hands clamping around her hips as he eased himself into her, filling her body, heart and soul.

The realization that she had never wanted a man the way she wanted Travis tore through her, frightening and exhilarating at the same time. Then he took up a rhythm, and all she could feel was him. Her release this time was an explosion that sent shock waves through her body, made all the more potent by the fact that Travis found his release right along with her. Within minutes, they fell asleep, wrapped around each other.

They awoke sometime before dawn and made love a second time. She fell back into a satiated slumber, pressed into Travis's side, knowing that her life would never be the same again.

THE EVENTS OF the night came rushing back as Chelsea awoke still in Travis's bed. Her gaze shot to the space where he'd slept, but the other side of the bed was empty. No sound came from anywhere else in the condo, either.

They had driven to Monterey together, and she knew Travis wouldn't abandon her. It wasn't a surprise to find a note from him next to a fresh pot of coffee saying he'd gone for a run on the beach. He was giving her time to wake up and go back to her own room, she knew.

She would never forget the night of passion they'd shared. He had driven her to heights she hadn't known existed. She didn't, couldn't, regret making love with him, but it didn't change anything. A part of her, a big part of her, was disappointed about that, but Travis had been honest with her from the beginning. This thing between them could go no further than the physical.

She poured her coffee and took it with her back into her bedroom.

Travis returned to the condo while she was in the shower. She heard him in his bedroom while she was getting dressed and packing to head home. She took her time getting ready, brushing her hair and applying her makeup and trying to tamp down her nervousness about seeing Travis after their night together.

When she walked into the living room, he was perched at the kitchen counter with his phone to his ear. His expression was serious, and when he waved her over and put the phone on speaker, she forgot all about her nerves. "Kevin, Chelsea is with me now."

"Good morning, Chelsea," Kevin's voice called through the phone.

"Morning." Chelsea shot Travis a questioning look.

"I was just telling Kevin about Peter admitting that he lied on the stand and agreeing to sign a statement saying so."

"It will take some work to iron out the logistics, but we'll get a lawyer started on it today," Kevin said.

"That's great. Thank you," Chelsea responded.

Travis cleared his throat. "Kevin and I were also discussing something else."

Chelsea had a feeling that *something else* was something she wasn't going to like.

"Even with Peter's statement, it's going to be an uphill climb getting the prosecutor to reopen the investigation," Kevin said gingerly.

She knew what Kevin said was true, but it didn't make it any less frustrating. "I sense you have an idea that may help."

"We have been talking," Travis jumped in, "and we

both think it will go a long way if we can get Lily's sister, Claire, to support reopening the case."

"I agree, but she has refused to speak to me."

"I know," Travis said, "but maybe with Peter retracting his statement, and knowing now there was another man in Lily's life, she will reconsider."

"Hey, I'm all for trying," Chelsea agreed.

"Good. Lily's sister lives in Santa Clarita. It would just be a little detour on the drive back to Los Angeles to stop in and see if she'll talk to us."

"I'm up for it," Chelsea said.

She was still high on having gotten Peter to admit to his falsehoods and relaxed from a night of incredible lovemaking. It felt like the tide might finally be turning in her and her dad's favor.

Chapter Twenty-Four

"This is it," Chelsea said, pointing to a mailbox with the address that they had for Claire Wong, Lily's half sister on their father's side. Claire had been twenty-two years old at the time of Lily's murder. She'd been in court every day of Chelsea's father's trial. Chelsea was sure the woman wouldn't be happy to see her, but she hoped Claire would be willing to listen. After all, if she was right, the wrong man was in jail for her sister's death. Claire had just as much incentive to get to the truth as Chelsea did.

Travis brought the car to a stop in front of a slightly rundown home surrounded by a good-size yard with mature trees and bushes. He and Chelsea sat in the car for a moment after he shut off the engine.

"Claire lived in LA at the time of Lily's death," Chelsea said. "She moved out here sometime after she inherited this place from her grandparents."

"It looks like it could use some TLC," Travis said.

"Claire was a community college student seven years ago. I don't know what she does now. Maybe she can't afford it."

"The background check I pulled on her had her employed at a small boutique in town." They sat in silence for another several seconds before Travis said, "Shall we?"

As they got out of the car, Chelsea noticed the curtains in the front window flutter. "Someone is inside, and they know we're here."

They walked up the front steps carefully since they appeared ready to crumble at any moment. The door opened before they had a chance to knock.

"What do you want?"

Claire Wong looked like a much older version of the young woman Chelsea had seen each day at her father's trial. The Claire standing in front of Chelsea now had aged two decades in the past seven years. Her pallor seemed to have a grayish tinge as if she didn't get enough sun. Her brown eyes and hair were dull and lackluster. She wore a sweater that was several sizes too big and jeans that did nothing to flatter.

Travis smiled at her. "Hi, we're sorry to bother you. We're looking for Claire Wong."

The woman's eyes flicked to Travis, then back to Chelsea. "Why? Who are you?"

"My name is Travis Collins."

"And my name is Chelsea Harper, although it used to be Chelsea Brooks."

Claire looked as if she had been slapped. "You're Franklin Brooks's daughter. I remember you now." She started to shut the door.

Chelsea slipped her hand around the door, stopping it from closing in their faces. "Please, we just want to talk," she said quickly.

"I don't care. I want you both to leave now."

"New information has come to light that exonerates my father. Don't you want to know the truth? Who really killed Lily?"

"Your father was convicted," Claire spat.

"What if the police, the prosecutor, everyone got it wrong? What if they just took the easy way out, and Lily's real killer has been walking free all this time? Since I started looking into my father's case, I've almost been run down, had my home broken into, and I've been shot."

Claire jolted, her eyes widening. "Oh, my God."

At least now she was listening. "That tells me someone doesn't want me looking into Lily's murder too hard, and I have to ask myself why that is."

Claire eyed Chelsea for a long moment. She prayed Claire was really thinking about what she had said.

Finally, Claire jerked her head at Travis. "Is he a cop?"

"I'm not a cop," he answered. "I'm a private investigator helping Chelsea get to the truth. We need your help in order to do that. Please."

After a moment, Claire opened the door and let them in. She led them to a kitchen table but didn't offer them anything to eat or drink. They sat.

"What do you want to know?" Claire asked hotly.

"Tell us about Lily," Travis said soothingly, taking the lead.

Claire visibly relaxed, a smile turning her mouth up and bringing some light into her eyes. "She was a great big sister. We had the same father, but he was never around for either of us. My mother died when I was nineteen, and Lily, she just jumped right in as a surrogate mother. Well, she'd always been somewhat of a surrogate mother. She was fifteen years older than me. I looked up to her like she was some sort of goddess." Claire laughed shortly. Then her smile fell, and her eyes hardened. "She was all I had, and your father took her from me."

"No," Chelsea said firmly. "I never believed that, and now I'm this close to proving it."

"How?" Claire crossed her arms over her chest, but a flicker of doubt flashed in her eyes. "What is this information you claim to have?"

Chelsea looked at Travis who nodded.

"We've learned that the eyewitness who said he saw my father leave Lily's house around the time of her murder lied."

Claire blinked, surprise widening her eyes. "Really."

"Yes," Chelsea answered. "He's agreed to sign a statement to that effect, too. He feels guilty for his part in putting my father in jail."

"That…that doesn't mean anything. It doesn't mean your father didn't kill Lily."

Travis interjected quickly, "We've also discovered that Lily likely had a new boyfriend whom no one ever questioned."

Claire's gaze moved away from Chelsea's face. Something about it struck Chelsea. "But you knew that already, right?" she asked.

Tears spilled down Claire's cheeks. "It doesn't matter. Your father killed Lily."

Chelsea fought the urge to reach across the table and slap the woman. She fisted her hands under the table.

Travis must have picked up on her anger. "Claire, do you know who Lily's new boyfriend was?" he asked softly.

Claire was quiet for so long Chelsea began to think she wouldn't answer. "No," she finally responded in a small voice. "She didn't tell me his name, and I never met him. Lily only said she had to be careful."

"Careful?" Travis pressed gently. "Why did Lily have to be careful?"

Claire shrugged. "I don't know. I didn't ask her."

"Did you tell the police this after Lily was killed?"

Chelsea asked, the anger in her voice too potent to conceal completely.

Claire noticed. "No," she said bitterly. "The cops said Franklin did it. I know he drank a lot, and he wanted to get back together with my sister, and she didn't want to. I didn't think it would help to throw some innocent guy to the cops."

"An innocent guy who didn't step forward after Lily, the woman he'd been dating, was murdered," Chelsea shot back. "Doesn't sound all that innocent to me."

"Telling the cops would have just muddied the waters," Claire said angrily. "They would have written Lily off as some promiscuous woman who got what she deserved. They had her killer, and I wasn't going to let him get away with it."

"The killer has gotten away with it," Chelsea said, acid in her voice. "For seven years while my dad sat in a jail cell because you didn't tell the truth."

Claire's eyes hardened. "How dare you? I loved my sister."

"Okay," Travis said. "Let's just everyone take a step back here. Breathe. We all want the same thing. To see Lily's killer pay for his crime."

Charged silence crackled between Chelsea and Claire. Lily's sister was just as bad as the cops and the prosecutor in her father's case. They'd all jumped to conclusions, and her father had paid the price.

"Lily may not have told you the name of the man she was seeing before she was killed, but is there anyone else she would have told?" Travis asked.

Claire pulled her gaze from Chelsea, but her scowl remained. "Maybe her best friend, Gina. But like I said,

Lily said she had to be careful, so I'm not sure if she told her, either."

"Do you still have any of Lily's belongings?" Travis asked. "Any old diaries or address books or anything where she might have mentioned this man?"

Claire hesitated. "I found an old diary of Lily's and some other things out at our father's place after he died."

"At your father's place? Why would she keep them there?" Travis asked.

Claire shrugged. "She lived with him for a while before she moved into her own place. Maybe she just forgot them."

"Would you mind if I took a look?"

Claire hesitated again. "I don't see how it could help." But she rose and disappeared into another part of the house.

"Are you okay?" Travis asked softly.

Chelsea shook her head but didn't give him any other response. She definitely wasn't okay. She didn't know what she was exactly. Livid at the authorities. Appalled at Claire's callousness with her father's life. She couldn't put her current state of mind into words. She wasn't sure there were any words to explain it.

Claire reappeared with a small box in her hands. "You can take it with you."

It was an obvious dismissal, but Chelsea didn't much care. She wanted to get out of this house and as far away from Claire as she could as soon as she could.

"But I'd like to have it back," Claire amended.

"I'll make sure you get it back as soon as possible," Travis assured her.

"I CAN'T BELIEVE HER." Chelsea said when Travis had driven away from Claire's house.

"I know that was hard to hear, but at least Claire confirmed for us that Lily did have a new man in her life. That was good. Hopefully something in this box will point to who he was."

"I can't wait until we get back to LA to look."

"Okay, how about I find us somewhere to eat, and we can see what's inside?"

They stopped at a diner about a mile from Claire's house. They ordered food, then Travis leaned over to look as Chelsea opened the box.

"A high school yearbook." Chelsea pulled it out. A bear was on the cover with his arms spread wide. A school year was embossed in gold between them. She flipped a few pages. She found Lily's graduation photo and stared for several long seconds before passing the yearbook to Travis.

"We should look at this more carefully later." He set the yearbook aside.

Chelsea reached back into the box and pulled out a small book. This one said *Diary* across the front. Chelsea opened the cover. The first entry was from January of the same year. She sighed dejectedly. "It's probably just her high school diary. It's not going to help us."

Travis took the diary from Chelsea's hands. "I don't know," he said, carefully flipping through pages. "I can understand why Lily may have left her high school yearbook at her father's place, but her diary? It seems like she would have taken it with her to make sure that her innermost thoughts stayed private."

Chelsea shrugged. "She was eighteen when she wrote it. Maybe she just forgot about it."

Travis turned another page. "She didn't forget." He slid the book over so Chelsea could see the date on the page he had open two thirds of the way into the diary. It was dated two months before Lily was killed.

The handwriting was more refined than in the earlier entries, but it was still clearly Lily's.

"It looks like she started writing in her diary again before she died. Maybe she left it at her father's because she was being careful, as her sister mentioned." Travis said.

Chelsea grabbed the book. She flipped through several pages. All of the ones toward the end were dated from that fall. She looked up at him, confused. "Why would Lily have felt she needed to be so careful?"

"My guess is if we read these entries, we'll find out."

She flipped to the end of the diary. "Usually I avoid spoilers, but I'll make an exception in this case. If Lily was having trouble with the new man in her life, and he killed her, her last entries will probably be the most telling."

Travis couldn't argue with her logic although he wanted to read the old diary carefully as soon as possible.

Chelsea scanned over the pages, reading quickly. "She was dating someone, but she didn't say his name. She only gives his initials. WR. She sounds worried." Travis watched as she swallowed hard. "She's worried about telling my dad about the new guy. How he will react," she said, her eyes not leaving the page.

"Does she say why?" Travis asked softly. If Lily was afraid of telling Franklin she was moving on, that gave support to the people who believed Franklin had killed her out of jealousy and possessiveness.

Chelsea didn't answer right away, but the book slid from her hands and onto the table. She turned to look at him, her eyes glazed over as if she'd been stunned.

"Chelsea, what is it?" He reached for the diary, which had fallen closed when she dropped it.

"Lily. She wrote that she was worried about how my

father would take it when he found out she was seeing his best friend. Bill Rowland," Chelsea murmured. "Travis, Lily's new boyfriend was my uncle Bill."

Chapter Twenty-Five

Uncle Bill opened the door and smiled when his gaze landed on Chelsea. It was a smile she couldn't return. She still couldn't bring herself to believe that her father's best friend had been sneaking around with Lily behind his back. There had to be another explanation. Something that didn't involve Uncle Bill betraying her father.

"Well, hello there. Isn't this a pleasant surprise?" Uncle Bill said.

"Uncle Bill, this is Travis Collins, the private investigator I hired to look into Dad's case."

"Nice to meet you, sir." Travis extended his hand.

Uncle Bill started for a moment, possibly surprised by Travis's formality. "Well, it's nice to meet you, too."

"I'm sorry for dropping by without calling first," Chelsea said, both anxious to get answers and terrified of them at the same time. "Do you have a minute to speak with us?"

"I always have time for you, sweetie. Come on in." Uncle Bill led them into the sunroom. "I'm taking advantage of every nice sunny day we have left."

His battered old recliner faced the glass wall of windows. Across from it was a matching love seat, slightly less worn. To his left was an end table with a pitcher of water and a coffee mug on top. The day's paper lay open on the seat of the recliner, clearly having been discarded there when he rose to answer the doorbell. Uncle Bill folded the paper along its creases and tossed it onto the floor before sitting.

She and Travis claimed the love seat.

"Sorry, I don't have any refreshments prepared right now. The market is on my list of things to do today. I can get you water if you'd like?" Uncle Bill made to get up, but Chelsea lifted a hand to stop him.

"That's okay. We're good."

"Okay," he said, sitting back into his recliner. "What can I do for you then?"

"You know I've been looking into Lily's murder," Chelsea said.

Uncle Bill nodded slowly. She could tell this was a subject he didn't want to talk about.

"Lily's sister finally agreed to talk to us. Lily wanted to keep it a secret because her new boyfriend was a friend of Dad's. She found Lily's diary after Dad's trial, and in it Lily mentions seeing a man whose initials were WR."

Uncle Bill's leg jiggled, and he wouldn't look at Chelsea. "I don't know what you're talking about."

"Sir, we could go back through your phone and computer records, if necessary, but it would be better for everyone, for Chelsea, if you told us the truth now," Travis said.

Chelsea suspected he was exaggerating. They didn't have any authority to obtain, much less search, Uncle Bill's computer, and nothing they'd uncovered to date was enough to compel the police to reopen her father's case.

But Uncle Bill didn't know that, and even if he did, tapping into his feelings for her seemed to do the trick.

He looked at her with eyes shining with tears. "Does your father know?"

Chelsea felt tears well in her own eyes. "No, and I'm not sure I'm going to tell him. It depends on what you tell me now."

"Nothing I can say will change anything."

"It will bring us one step closer to finding the truth, sir," Travis said.

Uncle Bill stared out the window for a long moment before answering. "Okay. What do you want to know?"

"How did your relationship with Lily begin?" Travis asked.

Chelsea was happy to let him take the lead questioning her uncle. She had too many emotions swirling through her to focus on asking the questions they needed answers to at the moment.

"We met when she and Franklin started dating. She was an amazing woman. Too good for Franklin. Too good for me as well."

"And when did the two of you begin your separate relationship?"

"Nothing happened until after Frank and Lily ended things."

"Did Lily end things with my dad because of you?" Chelsea chimed in, bitterness lacing each syllable.

"No. Lily wasn't that kind of woman. She was faithful to your dad even when he wasn't faithful to her," Uncle Bill spat. His gaze flashed with anger that Chelsea met with anger of her own.

"Okay," Travis said in a quelling tone. "How long was it after Lily and Franklin broke up that you two got together?"

"I don't know," Uncle Bill said, shifting his gaze to

Travis. "You have to understand Franklin was very vol-
atile during those days. He was drinking and stepping
out on Lily a lot. We were both concerned about him.
He'd always been a heavy drinker, but it had gotten so
much worse, and neither of us knew what to do about it.
We tried talking to him, but he would just get angry. We
spent a lot of time commiserating, and one thing led to
another." Uncle Bill's eyes shifted back to Chelsea. "But
like I said, nothing happened until it was over between
Lily and Franklin."

He seemed sincere, but Chelsea wasn't sure she could
believe him. After all, he'd been lying to her for the past
seven years.

"You visited Lily at her home, correct?" Travis said,
pulling Uncle Bill's attention back to him.

"Sometimes, yes."

"What about the night she was killed? Were you two
still together then?" Chelsea asked. All the fire seemed to
have gone out of Uncle Bill. He stared down at the tiled
sunroom floor. "We were."

"Did you tell the police about your relationship after
Lily was killed?" Chelsea asked.

Uncle Bill looked up. "No," he answered, his voice
small.

"So, you just let Dad take the fall?" Disgust at the man
sitting in front of her swept through her body. She hadn't
known him at all.

Uncle Bill looked at her, his eyes imploring. "I didn't
kill Lily. I may be a coward for not telling the cops about
my relationship with her, but I did not kill her."

"Where were you the night Lily was murdered?" Travis asked.

"I'll never forget it. I was out with my employees. Celebrating the opening of my second shop. I would have loved to have Lily there with me, but we were still taking things slow. Keeping our relationship to ourselves so we didn't hurt Franklin." Uncle Bill stared out of the windows again, but this time it was clear he was looking into the past. "He was supposed to be there, too, but he never showed up."

Probably because he was meeting with Lily. It was the perfect time, since Lily would have known that Bill wouldn't show up to interrupt them.

"So, you think Franklin might have killed Lily?" Travis returned to his questioning.

Uncle Bill shrugged. "I don't know. He was a mean drunk, but I had never seen him be violent toward anyone. But who else could it have been?"

"Maybe Lily had a third boyfriend?" Chelsea said bitterly.

Uncle Bill's expression turned to surprise as if he'd never even considered the possibility. But if Lily had been playing around with her father and Uncle Bill, it was more than possible she had other companions. It seemed she wasn't as nice as she led everyone to believe she was.

"Did you know if Lily was having difficulties with anyone specific?" Travis asked.

Uncle Bill's forehead crinkled. "What do you mean?"

"We were told she had a vandalism incident and a possible break-in at her place."

"Oh, yeah. I think she mentioned something like that. But nothing came of it. Probably just kids messing around."

"Did she ever find out who did it?"

"If she did, I don't remember. You might try asking her neighbor. Kind of a busybody." Uncle Bill rolled his eyes. "Knew everything that happened in the neighborhood."

"Gina McGrath?" Travis asked.

"Gina? No." Uncle Bill shook his head. "I was talking about the guy. John. Justin. Something starting with a *J*. He was always in Lily's business."

"Jace," Chelsea supplied the name.

"Maybe," Uncle Bill said, sounding unsure. "It's been too long for me to be certain."

Chelsea shot a glance at Travis, but his gaze was locked on Bill's face.

"Lily thought he was a nice, if somewhat lonely, guy," Uncle Bill continued, "but he gave me the creeps."

"He did? Why?" Travis pressed.

"Well, he was always finding reasons to come over to Lily's place. And more than once, I caught him looking at her from the windows of his house."

A spidery feeling crawled down Chelsea's back.

Uncle Bill snapped his fingers. "If you ask me the cops should have taken a much harder look at that guy."

Chapter Twenty-Six

Travis spoke to Kevin on speaker as he drove away from Bill Rowland's house.

"So, Franklin's best friend was seeing Lily at the time of her death. Man, that is some friend," Kevin summarized the information Travis had just conveyed.

Travis cut a look at Chelsea who still seemed to be in a state of shock. "Chelsea's in the car with me."

"Oh, sorry, Chelsea," Kevin apologized.

"No, you're right. I'm struggling to wrap my mind around how Uncle Bill could have done this to my dad."

"We will need to check on Bill's alibi for the night of the murder," Travis said.

Kevin groaned. "Confirming a seven-year-old alibi. Give me something hard, why don't you?"

"Sorry." Travis stopped at a corner to let a jogger cross the street before making a right-hand turn. "Bill Rowland swears he had nothing to do with Lily's death but—"

"But he's been lying for nearly a decade, so we can't trust anything he has said," Chelsea interrupted.

Travis stole a glance at her. She was focused on the scenery outside the passenger window, avoiding his gaze.

"Bill gave us the names of the employees he remembers being at the party the night of the murder. Some of them no longer work for him, so they don't have a strong incentive to lie for him if they were ever inclined to do so." Travis ordered the virtual assistant on his phone to send the list of names to Kevin. Seconds later, he heard a faint ping come from the other side of the line.

"Got it," Kevin said. "I'll get started on running down this alibi. What are you going to do?"

"I think the most important thing right now is to focus on the information Bill gave us," Travis said, slowing to a stop at a red light. "If Jace Orson was at home the night Lily died, and he lied about it, we need to know why."

"Agreed," Kevin said.

"I'm going to drop Chelsea off at her house, and then I'll come into the office," Travis replied.

"Wait, what?" Chelsea finally tore her attention away from the window to look at him. "Drop me off? No way."

"Guys, I'm going to hang up," Kevin said before quickly ending the call.

"Chelsea, Jace Orson might not be involved at all." But Travis's gut was telling him that wasn't the case. "But if he is, he's probably the person who tried to run you down and vandalized your home and shot at you. He's dangerous."

"He's dangerous to you, too, then."

"But I'm trained to deal with dangerous people, and you aren't. You hired me for a reason. Let me do my job."

She looked like she wanted to argue with him. Instead, she pressed her lips together tightly.

"Listen." He tried a different approach. "I'll reach out to Jace again. When we spoke to him, we weren't thinking about him as a suspect in Lily's murder. I'll see how he responds to the suggestion that he lied about where he was the night of the murder. Maybe there is some innocent explanation."

"You don't believe that, or you would take me with you to talk to him." She was too astute for her own good.

"There is a lot West can do, but ultimately we have to turn this case over to the cops and the prosecutor if you want to get your dad out of prison. Let me do my job. I'll let you know what's happening as soon as I can."

Chelsea stayed silent, the tension building in the car to the point he couldn't stand it anymore.

"I can't take the chance that you'll get hurt again if something goes wrong," he said softly. "You've already been shot. I can't—I don't think I could survive it."

Chelsea hesitated for a beat longer. "Okay. I'll sit home twiddling my thumbs."

He let out a sigh of relief and a bark of laughter at the same time. "I doubt that. Actually, I was thinking you could call your cousin, Victor, and have him stay with you."

"Stay with me?"

"I don't want you to be alone. Maybe Victor could help you finish painting."

Now Chelsea laughed. "You don't know Victor. Painting would be the last thing he'd want to do, but I will call him."

She made the call while he drove. Victor was waiting for them in front of Chelsea's house when they pulled up a little while later.

Travis put the car in Park but didn't shut off the engine.

Instead of getting out of the car, Chelsea grabbed his forearm. "This feels like one of those moments in the movies when the hero goes off to face the bad guy and doesn't come back."

He lifted a hand and caressed her cheek. "This is not a movie, and I'm no hero."

"I beg to differ with that last part." She leaned forward and placed a fast, hard kiss on his lips. "Promise me you'll be careful and come back to me safe."

He knew it was a fool's promise. Nothing was ever certain in life. But if it alleviated even a moment of her worry, he also knew he'd make that promise a million times over. "I promise."

It was a promise he had every intention of keeping.

Chapter Twenty-Seven

Damn. Damn. Damn. He had been reduced to sneaking into his own house through the back door. It had been all he could do to control his temper and not slam the door as he went in. The last thing he needed was to draw more attention to himself. His neighbors kept to themselves for the most part, but he had no idea who else Chelsea and her private investigator had spoken to. Whether they'd spread their suspicions about him to his neighbors. But he knew they were looking for him. He knew that they knew, or at least suspected, he killed Lily.

He shuddered. Thinking about how it would feel to have everyone know that he killed Lily. They'd look at him the way they looked at Franklin Brooks. Worse than the way they looked at him. The rage was threatening to take over again, but this time he didn't try to stop it. He didn't want to control it anymore.

He headed into his bedroom and went straight for the closet. Pushing aside the clothes folded neatly on the overhead shelf, he exposed two boxes. One held his mementos. The other his gun. Chelsea had left him no choice. His life as he knew it was over. But that didn't mean he couldn't exact some revenge before it all exploded for good.

He took the gun from its case, holding it for a moment,

feeling the steel in his hand, its weight and balance. Then he slid in a loaded magazine.

He'd given Chelsea Harper the chance to walk away before.

He wouldn't give her that chance this time.

Chapter Twenty-Eight

Chelsea took a step back and eyed the newly painted living room walls. It had taken her and Victor the better part of the evening to paint over the walls with the light blue shade that she'd selected, but she liked the results.

Chelsea set her roller down on a piece of newspaper. "Ready to start doing the trim?"

Victor groaned. "We don't have to do it all in one day."

"I want to get my house back together. And I don't want to have to prep the room a second time just to do the trim."

Victor groaned again, shooting a glance at the sand and eggshell paint cans. "Well, can we at least take a break? The pizza will be here soon, and I'm starving."

"Okay, but after we eat, we knock this trim out. I want to get my home back."

The sound of gunfire burst from the television speakers, drawing their attention. Their pending project would have taken considerably less time if Victor hadn't brought along the *Dark Knight* trilogy on DVD. She and her cousin shared a love of action and superhero films, and even though they'd seen the Christian Bale movies nearly half a dozen times each, Chelsea loved watching them again with her cousin.

Victor's attention was glued to the television, but Chelsea's eye landed on a white envelope she hadn't noticed on the television stand earlier.

"Hey, what is this?" she asked, crossing the room and picking up the envelope.

Victor glanced over at her, then back to the television. "Oh, it was wedged between your screen door and your front door when I got here. It must have been delivered while you were staying with Travis."

"Yeah, I guess." She turned the envelope over. The return address was for a law firm in San Diego.

Victor cleared his throat.

Chelsea pulled her gaze from the envelope to look at her cousin. "What?"

"About Travis."

"What about Travis?"

"I know you're a grown woman, but I worry about you. You're my cousin, and you're like a sister to me. I don't want to see you hurt again."

"Travis is nothing like Simon."

Victor held his hands out. "I'm not saying he is. Just that it seems like the two of you have grown close. This investigation is a lot. You're close to maybe finally proving your father's innocence, and that could leave you emotionally vulnerable."

"Emotionally vulnerable?" Chelsea teased.

"Ugh, I mean the last thing I want to do is talk to you about your romantic life. Just know that if that man hurts you, he will have to answer to me."

Chelsea smiled and threw her arms around her cousin. "You know how much I love you, don't you?"

Victor squeezed her in a tight bear hug. "I do. And I love you, too."

The doorbell rang, signaling the arrival of their pizza. "I'll get it." Victor stepped out of the embrace.

"I'll grab some paper plates for us," Chelsea said, heading for the kitchen while opening the envelope she still held in her hand. She stopped just inside the kitchen, shocked at the information in the letter.

Her father-in-law had made her a beneficiary in his will. The letter was brief and didn't get into details about exactly what she'd inherited, but it invited her to reach out to the lawyers to discuss the issue more fully as soon as possible.

So, this was why Simon had been so desperate to talk to her. She wondered if he knew what she had inherited. She was debating whether to call the lawyers right then when Victor screamed, "Chelsea! Run!"

There was a loud crack, a groan and then a thump.

Someone was in her house.

Despite Victor's order to run, her feet felt as if they were glued to the ground. Her brain finally sent the message to move, but she knew she couldn't just leave Victor. "Victor?" She started for the front door.

He was lying face down on the floor in front of the door. The man standing over him looked up.

Jace Orson.

Jace smiled at her, and her stomach twisted into knots. "Chelsea. Good to see you again."

She turned and ran back into the kitchen. Jace's footsteps pounded on the hardwood floors behind her. She grabbed at a counter drawer, reached inside and pulled out a knife.

"Ah, ah, ah. I wouldn't do that if I were you."

She turned to find Jace pointing a gun at her.

"Put down the knife, Chelsea."

She didn't have any choice. A knife couldn't beat a bullet. Her shoulder throbbed at the memory of having been shot. Jace was even closer now. If he pulled the trigger, he wouldn't just graze her this time. It would be a direct hit.

The knife clattered as she let it drop to the countertop.

"Good girl. Now come here."

She didn't move.

Jace crossed the kitchen in three long strides. "I said come here!" He grabbed her arm, wrenching it behind her back in a painful twist, and pulled her tightly against his chest. "From here on out, you do exactly what I tell you. Do you understand?"

Her eyes filled with tears of terror. She nodded.

"Say it!" Jace yelled.

"Ye-yes," she stammered.

"Good. Now move."

"My cousin... He needs help."

"The guy at the door? He'll be fine. At least he will be as long as you do what you're told."

"You didn't... Is he?" A different kind of fear flooded through her.

"He's not dead. I told you he's fine for now. I just needed him out of the way to get to you." Jace pulled on her injured arm drawing a wince forcing her forward. "We need to go."

"I'm not going anywhere with you." She struggled against him.

"No?" Jace yanked her into the hallway where Victor still lay on the floor not moving. "Maybe I'll have to show you how serious I am." He pointed the gun at Victor's head.

"No! No, I'll go with you." If going with Jace kept Victor safe, kept him alive, she'd go. She would trade Victor's life for hers.

She let Jace push her forward, stepping over Victor's prone form and out the front door. Travis would come for her. She just had to do everything she could to stay alive until he did.

THE WEST SECURITY AND INVESTIGATIONS offices were busy with activity when Travis arrived. He'd gone to Jace's house before heading to the office, but no one answered. It looked like he hadn't been there for a couple of days, which didn't necessarily mean anything, but Travis's instincts were buzzing. They were onto something.

The first thing he did when he got back to the office was request a rush background check on Jace Orson. The company they worked with was good and promised to have something to him within two hours. He also tried calling Jace at his accounting firm, but his boss said he hadn't heard from Jace in days.

Travis spent the next couple hours calling Bill Rowland's alibi witnesses for the night of Lily's murder. He'd just gotten off the phone with one of them when his computer dinged with an incoming email. Jace Orson's background report. He read it quickly, then printed out a copy before hurrying into Kevin's office.

"I think I got something." Travis handed the report to him.

"What is it?" Kevin flipped through the pages, scanning.

"Jace Orson has a red Mazda registered in his name." He reached across the desk and helped Kevin flip to the relevant page. "Chelsea and I saw him get out of that vehicle the day we met him. But he also has a black Oldsmobile in his name."

Kevin made the connection instantly. He looked up

from the pages in his hand with a sparkle in his eye that said they'd just hit on something significant. "Just like the car that tried to run down Chelsea."

"Exactly," Travis responded excitedly.

"Okay, it adds to the questions we want to ask Mr. Orson, but it doesn't exactly help us find him."

That, unfortunately, was true.

"Did you find a second residence? Maybe a family member's place where he might be staying?" Kevin handed the papers back to Travis.

"No," Travis said, his frustration doubling. "Both of Orson's parents are deceased. He's an only child. The Oldsmobile was his mother's. It looks like he inherited it when she died three years ago, but the registration is still active, so it's likely he has it stored somewhere."

"Could be in a paid parking spot or in a self-storage unit. If he used it in a hit-and-run, he wouldn't want to park it in his driveway where everyone could see it. That could also be where he's hiding out. Assuming he is hiding out," Kevin added pointedly. "He could just as easily be at a conference or on vacation."

Travis shook his head. "I checked with the IT firm where he works on my way back to the office from his house. He hasn't been in for the last three days. He didn't call in sick or arrange for time off. He probably won't have a job when, if, he shows up."

"So, he's nuking his life." Kevin frowned. The concern in his tone was unmistakable, and Travis shared it.

"Yes." If Jace was at the point where he no longer cared about showing up for work or at his house, he might feel like he had nothing left to lose. That could mean he was desperate, and desperate people were very dangerous. "But it gets worse. The IT firm is a state contractor. I recognized the company's name from my time with the LAPD. They provide the IT guys for the police department's help desk. Orson's boss told me that Orson was assigned to the Hollywood police station until early this year."

"So, Orson had access to all the LAPD's police files."

Travis nodded. "It's possible. I'd even go so far as to say, given what we now know, that he knew Chelsea was looking into her father's case."

Kevin stroked his chin. "It wouldn't be hard for a computer technician to tag a file, so he's notified when it was accessed."

"No, it wouldn't be hard at all," Travis agreed.

"Okay, well, all we can do is keep searching for him," Kevin said, turning back to his computer. "In the meantime, we've got an attorney working on the affidavit for Peter Schmeichel. He's hopeful that it will be done by the end of the week or early next at the latest."

Travis frowned. That gave Peter plenty of time to change his mind. He hoped that didn't happen. Peter seemed remorseful about his lies.

"I reached out to three of the nearly dozen names Rowling gave me," Kevin said. "They all remembered the party and confirmed that, to the best of their recollection, Bill was at the party the whole night. One person was even able to send me photos of Bill with a dozen other people. The metadata from those photos confirms the dates and times Bill gave us."

"That's a pretty airtight alibi."

"Yeah, I'm not feeling Rowland for a murderer," Travis responded.

"But you are feeling Jace Orson?"

The knot in Travis's chest twisted tighter. "I am. Now we just have to prove it."

His phone rang, and he plucked it out of his pocket. "Hello?" The voice on the other end spoke so fast that it took him a moment to realize it was Victor, Chelsea's cousin. "Victor, slow down. I can't understand what you're saying."

"It's Chelsea. She's been... I think she's been kidnapped."

JACE PUSHED CHELSEA toward his car, the barrel of the gun pressed into her back. He opened the passenger door and shoved her over the middle console and into the driver's seat before climbing into the passenger seat himself. He handed her the keys and ordered, "Drive."

She started the engine without protest and pulled from the driveway, praying some nosy neighbor was watching her be kidnapped and was on the phone at that very moment calling out the cavalry. She gripped the steering wheel with white knuckles, her entire body on alert as she assessed her situation.

It was dire. Jace held the gun below the view of the window but pointed it at her with his finger on the trigger. His eyes were on the road.

"Where are we going?"

"Just drive," he responded.

So, she did. When they neared the interchange for an older, underused stretch of road, he directed her to it. "Make this right."

She did as she was told, still trying to formulate a plan. It was late, and the old highway had seen a drop in traffic since the nearby freeway had been built. She hoped someone had seen her kidnapping and called the cops, but she couldn't count on it. If she wanted to get out of this situation alive, she'd have to do it on her own.

She took a deep breath, trying to remain calm and focus on finding a solution. Her first order of business was making sure Jace didn't just decide to kill her and be done with her. He had, she was sure now, killed Lily, but she still had no real idea why. Maybe if she could get him talking, she could get an answer and distract him enough so that she could get away.

She swallowed the ball of terror in her throat and spoke. "You killed Lily."

Jace's body stiffened, but he didn't respond.

Chelsea continued, "You killed her, and you let my father take the blame for her murder. Why?"

"He deserved it. He never treated my Lily like she should have been treated. Like the treasure she was. I tried to tell her she deserved better."

"You tried to tell her?" She remembered he'd said something similar the day she and Travis met him.

"I thought she understood. She broke up with him, but then she started dating that other guy."

Uncle Bill. "Is that why you killed her? Because she wouldn't date you?"

"She was mine."

"She was her own person. She belonged to herself, and she didn't deserve what you did to her," Chelsea growled, forgetting her fear for a moment. She glanced away from the road to take a look at Jace.

He showed no remorse at all. His eyes were cold and emotionless. Empty. "She was mine, and now she is mine forever." He stared out the front windshield, his voice eerily calm.

That was probably as close to a confession as she was

likely to get from him. His calmness was the most ter-
rifying part of her current ordeal. Jace didn't seem to be
bothered in the least at having killed Lily. Just like he
wouldn't be bothered at all by killing Chelsea.

Her pulse raced as an almost uncontrollable urge to get
out of the car and as far away from the monster beside
her racked her body with tremors. But she needed to keep
calm and clearheaded if she had any hope of surviving
this. Jace had eluded justice for seven years. He might be
a sick monster, but he wasn't stupid. She had to keep him
talking until she had a plan.

"So, what now? You can't hope to get away. The private investigator I've been working with knows you killed
Lily. The cops probably know I'm missing by now and are
looking for me." She hoped that part was true. "They'll
realize that you kidnapped me sooner rather than later."

Jace finally showed some sign of emotion, his face
twisting into a mask of rage. "Just keep driving and shut
up!" His fury blew through the car.

Chelsea stopped talking. She'd blown it, and now he
was going to have to drive to some remote area and kill
her. Well, she wouldn't go down without a fight.

Several minutes passed in silence. They crested a hill,
and Chelsea saw headlights shining a dozen yards in front
of them. A hasty, dangerous plan formed in her head.
There was no time to think it through.

As the truck passed by them, she slammed on the
brakes, her seat belt yanking her back sharply. Jace jerked
forward, too, the gun flying from his hands and landing
on the floor well in front of him. His head banged against
the dashboard.

She wasted no time throwing the car door open and

running toward the truck. It had already passed by them, but their sudden stop had the truck slowing. She ran.

She heard the passenger door to the car open behind her and a gunshot ring out.

Chapter Twenty-Nine

Travis's heart raced. He was more afraid than he had ever been in his life. Victor had calmed down enough on the phone to explain that he'd opened Chelsea's door to a man pointing a gun toward him. After he'd yelled out a warning to Chelsea, he'd been knocked out. When he'd come to, Chelsea and the man were gone. Victor had gotten a quick look at the car the man drove, and although he didn't get the license plate, the description matched Jace's red Mazda.

A patrol car was already at Chelsea's house, but Kevin drove Travis to the police station. Travis burst into the police conference room and barked, "What do you know?"

Detective Owens rose from his seat as did the other man at the conference table.

"You can't just come bursting in here, Collins!" Lieutenant Zach Grady blustered. Grady had been in charge of the precinct while Travis was a cop. They hadn't gotten along even before Travis went to Internal Affairs about his dirty colleagues.

"Slow down, Travis," Owens said, stepping between him and Grady. "We are already doing everything that can be done. The BOLO is out. Squad cars all over the city are on alert. I notified the state police myself, and they're combing the interstate. They're also standing by to offer any other support we might need." He put a hand on either of Travis's shoulders. "We'll find her."

That was all fine and good, but Owens hadn't answered Travis's question. How had Jace gotten to Chelsea in the first place?

"How did this happen?" Travis bit out again.

Owens looked at the lieutenant and got a nod from his boss before answering. "It looks like Jace got the jump on Chelsea's cousin."

Travis vibrated with anger.

"When Victor Harper came to, he called it in. We got there quickly and set up a perimeter, but we think Jace had a ten- to fifteen-minute head start on us."

Ten to fifteen minutes. It didn't sound like much, but a car could turn that into significant distance. Especially since they didn't have a clue where Jace was heading.

"Mr. Harper is in the hospital. He probably has a concussion, but he'll be okay." Owens darted a look at the lieutenant.

"What?" Kevin asked, looking between the two police officers.

"Mr. Harper was pistol-whipped," Owens answered.

Pistol-whipped. Jace had a gun. So, Chelsea might already be—

Travis wouldn't let himself think about it. Except he couldn't stop. Chelsea had been kidnapped by an obsessed killer. A man who had already killed once and who probably knew the authorities knew it. He had nothing to lose by exacting revenge and killing Chelsea.

Don't hurt her. Please don't hurt her.

But Jace would. That was his plan. To kill Chelsea.

Travis had to find them first.

"Like Owens said, we're doing everything humanly possible to find Ms. Harper," Grady chimed in.

"You have someone at Jace's house?" Travis asked.

Grady nodded. "We're executing a search warrant now."

Travis turned for the door, stopping only when Owens grabbed his arm. "Where do you think you're going?"

"To Orson's house to help with the search."

Owens shook his head. "You know you can't be there."

"Chelsea and I have been looking into Lily Wong's case. I have more insight into this guy now than either of you do. I may see something that clues us in to where he's taking her that your guys won't."

Owens looked at Grady again, an entire conversation taking place between the longtime colleagues without a word spoken.

Finally, Grady nodded again. "You can't touch anything," he said to Travis before turning to Owens. "Go with him."

Orson's house was swarming with officers when Travis and Owens arrived. Travis was out of the car before Owens shut off the engine. They stepped inside the house together.

Travis forced himself to take several deep breaths and think. People were creatures of habit. There had to be something in the house that hinted at Jace's plan. He had to find it. He walked through the house with Owens, touching nothing just as Grady had directed. He didn't need to touch anything. Not yet anyway. He needed to get a feel for how Jace lived first. How he used the space. That was likely to tell him where Jace would hide anything of value.

As he did, he thought about Chelsea. She was a fighter.

She had proven that by fighting for her dad when everyone, including him, thought it was a lost cause.

Owens spoke quietly to one of the officers in the hall. When he returned, Travis knew the news wasn't good. "So far they haven't found anything, but we aren't done looking."

Ignoring Lieutenant Grady's admonishment to look and not touch, Travis went to Orson's bedroom.

The officer searching the room spun around as he entered. "Hey, you can't be here!"

Owens stepped into the room behind Travis with his badge out. "It's okay, Officer Johnson," Owens read the name on the officer's chest. "He's with me. Why don't you go help in the basement?"

Officer Johnson trotted out of the bedroom.

Travis marched to the nightstand and yanked the door open.

Owens didn't say a word about Travis ignoring the lieutenant's instructions. Instead, he went to the closet and picked up searching where Officer Johnson had left off. After a few minutes, he called, "Hey, I think I've got something."

Owens pulled a metal box from the closet and set it on the bed as Travis walked over to join him. The box had a flimsy lock. Owens borrowed a flashlight from one of the officers in another room, and with two solid hits, the lock gave way.

Inside were photographs. Hundreds of them of Lily from years ago and dozens that had been taken more recently. Of Chelsea. There were even a few photographs of Travis. Orson had clearly been watching them. Of course he had.

"This is creepy," Owens said. "Jace was stalking Lily Wong."

"And Chelsea," Travis added.

The detective's cell phone rang. "Owens." He was silent for a moment, then said, "Lieutenant, I'm going to put you on speaker so Travis can hear." Owens hit a button on the screen. "Okay, Lieutenant. Go ahead."

"We just got a call from a driver out on Old Route 1. They said they passed a red Mazda, and a woman jumped out. Followed by a man with a gun. The passerby reported shots fired."

Travis went numb. "Chelsea. Is she—"

"The driver who called it in said a man shot at his truck. The bullet didn't hit him or his vehicle, but it scared him. He drove off but called it in as soon as he was sure the shooter wasn't following him."

"So, we don't know if Chelsea—" Travis started.

Lieutenant Grady cut him off. "I've got units rolling in the direction that the man said the car was headed. And the state police are putting a chopper in the air."

Travis looked at Owens.

Owens pulled his keys from his coat pocket. "I'll drive."

CHELSEA THREW HERSELF onto the paved highway. Tires screeched, and she lifted her head in time to see the truck tear off down the highway. Tears rolled down her cheeks as she watched the brakes fade into darkness.

Then Jace was there beside her.

"Get up," he ordered.

She looked up into the barrel of the gun. She stood.

He grabbed her arm and turned her around roughly, so her back was to him. The cold metal of the gun pressed against her temple. His breath touched her cheek, his voice pure rage. "I should shoot you right now but I'm not going to make the same mistake I made with Lily. When I'm finished with you nobody will ever find your body."

She didn't want to die. Not when she was so close to freeing her dad. Not at the hands of the man who had destroyed both of their lives. And not when she had finally found someone, she could see having a future with.

"Pl-please, no," she stammered.

"Don't worry. I have plans to make you pay for ruining my life. You don't deserve a quick death. Now, get back in the car. Move!"

Shaking uncontrollably, she walked with him to the car. Again, he directed her to the passenger side and pushed her over behind the wheel.

"Drive!" he yelled, pressing the gun into her side hard enough to make her yelp.

She got the car moving again.

"Faster! You just made a huge mistake. And I'm going to make sure you pay for it."

"You don't have to do this."

"I'm not going to jail."

"You didn't have any problem letting my father go to jail," Chelsea said, fury rising in her.

"Just shut up and drive!" Jace screamed.

The hysteria in his tone was enough to temper her fury and ignite another wave of fear. She knew she shouldn't antagonize him any further. Her attempt to escape hadn't gone the way she hoped, but the driver of the truck had gotten away. Surely, he had called the police. She just had to hang in there for a little longer.

They'd driven another several miles when she noticed the flashing lights in her rearview mirror. Jace noticed them at the same time.

"Faster." He slammed his hand down on her right thigh in an attempt to push the accelerator to the floor. The car sped up, but the next time she checked the rearview mirror, the flashing blue lights were closer and had doubled.

A voice came over the police cruiser's speaker. "Pull over."

"Don't," Jace said through gritted teeth.

She didn't stop the car, but she slowed. She wasn't sure what the cops knew. Did they know Jace was holding her against her will? Or had they only been told about a man who had shot at another driver? Would they open fire at the car with her in it?

She eased up on the accelerator even more.

"Don't stop." Jace reached across the car again, this time grabbing the wheel. The car veered across the center line in the road.

Chelsea yanked the wheel in the other direction, but she overcompensated. They went off the road completely this time, hitting the ditch beyond the shoulder.

Jace screamed next to her.

All four wheels left the ground for a brief moment, and then they were rolling. Once. Twice. The windshield cracked, and the driver window shattered into hundreds of pieces, scattering glass over the front seats.

Chelsea was completely disoriented, unsure which way was up as the car finally came to a stop.

Jace moaned.

She turned her head slowly, but pain still exploded in her skull. The car was upside down, balanced on its top, but their seat belts held both of them strapped to their seats. Yet somehow Jace had managed to hold on to the gun.

Chelsea's eyes widened, her pain forgotten as he raised the gun and pointed it in her direction.

OWENS AND TRAVIS rounded a curve in the highway, and Travis quickly took in the scene. The Mazda was fishtailing, swerving from one side of the road to the other before it dropped into the ditch at the side of the road. The sickening crash of metal nearly stopped his heart.

Travis watched in terror as the car rolled several times before coming to a stop. "Chelsea!" he screamed, opening his car door before Owens came to a complete stop, and raced toward the accident. The police cruiser that had been following along with them pulled over on the opposite shoulder of the road. Travis drew his gun as he raced past it, pushing aside the nearly paralyzing thought that Chelsea might be dead.

She wasn't dead. She couldn't be dead.

But she could be badly injured. The crash was bad. The Mazda was upside down.

He got to the driver's side of the car and knelt. Chelsea was in there, but the passenger seat was empty. "Chelsea? Baby, answer me, please?"

Chelsea turned her head slowly toward him. "Jace. He got out. Ran away."

"Don't worry about him. We'll get him."

A shot rang out, shattering the back window that had somehow remained intact after the crash.

Chelsea screamed.

Travis ducked down behind the rear of the car. "Jace! Give it up! You're surrounded."

But Orson clearly had no intention of giving up. Travis could hear him moving through the trees and shrubbery on the other side of the ditch. If he got enough distance between himself and the road, he stood a good chance of getting away.

Travis went back to the driver's-side window. "Chelsea, I'll be back. Hang in there for me, baby," he said, and then he took off after Orson.

Orson was fast, but Travis was motivated. He wasn't going to let him get away.

Orson pushed through the branches with Travis right behind, closing the distance. Travis put on a burst of speed and threw himself at Jace's back, slamming the man onto the pine-needle-covered ground. Jace's gun flew out to the side.

Anger flooded through Travis's body. He flipped Orson onto his stomach and drove his fist into the killer's face. He had never been so enraged or scared. This man was a killer. He had kidnapped Chelsea, and he probably planned to kill her.

Orson struggled, but Travis used his weight to hold him down while he pounded his fist into the monster's face. He wasn't sure how many times he hit him before he felt someone pulling him away.

"Travis, stop. Enough."

Owens dragged him off Orson. A second officer grabbed Jace's arms and slapped cuffs on his wrists.

"Go back to Chelsea," Owens ordered. "The EMTs got her out of the car, and they're about to transfer her to the ER."

Travis didn't have to be told twice. He backtracked through the woods at a run. "Chelsea!" he called as he cleared the trees. He spotted the gurney being lifted into the ambulance and raced forward. "Chelsea!" He ignored the EMT's protest as he hauled himself into the back of the ambulance.

"Sir, you can't be in here," the EMT said with a glower.

"It's okay. I want him here," Chelsea said.

The EMT shrugged and closed the back door and called to the driver to get them moving.

Travis sat on the bench across from the gurney and stroked Chelsea's cheek while the paramedic started an intravenous line in her arm.

"Hey, you're going to be okay, Chels." Travis leaned down and kissed her on the lips. "I have never been more afraid in my life. When I saw your car flipped over—"

She took his hand and squeezed. "I'm okay. Did you get him?"

Travis squeezed back. "We got him. He won't hurt anyone else ever again."

She sighed. "Then it's over. My father—"

"It will take a little more time, but your father is coming home." Travis stroked her cheek. "You did it, Chels. You got the truth and freed your father."

THE LAST SIX hours had taken Travis on a roller coaster of emotion, but the doctors had checked out both Victor and Chelsea and declared no permanent damage had been done to either. The cousins would be spending the night in the hospital, though. It had taken Victor, Chelsea and a doctor to get Brenda Harper to go home and get some rest, but she'd finally relented. Now it was time for Travis to do what he knew had to be done and say goodbye to Chelsea.

"They aren't going to let me out until tomorrow," Chelsea said, sounding displeased when he entered her hospital room.

"Well, I'm sure the doctors know what's best."

Chelsea pushed herself up straighter in the bed. "I was thinking that I could make dinner for us tomorrow when I get home. It would be nice to get back in my own kitchen."

She reached a hand out to him, but he didn't move closer to the bed to take it.

"You should probably rest when you get home," he said in a flat voice that sounded nothing like his own.

Chelsea let her hand fall to the mattress. "What's wrong?"

"Listen, Chelsea. We got the evidence you need to prove your father's innocence. Orson is in jail. West Investigations will work with you to get whatever evidence you need to the prosecutor."

"Oh." The hurt look that crossed her face nearly crushed him.

Silence fell.

"I told you I don't do the relationship thing," he said quietly.

"Yes, you did. If that's what you want, I guess that's it."

His heart felt like it was being squeezed in a vise. He wished he could be different, but it wouldn't be fair to either one of them.

"Thank you for everything," she said quietly.

"If you ever need anything, just call, okay? Anytime, day or night. I'll be there."

"Goodbye, Travis."

"Goodbye, Chelsea." He forced himself to turn away from the bed before she could see the tears welling in his eyes and walked out of the room.

You did the right thing, he repeated as he walked to his car and drove home.

Then why did it hurt so much?

Chapter Thirty

A week had passed since Chelsea had been released from the hospital. There was still a lot to do before her father was released from prison, but the prosecutor's office had filed the necessary paperwork with the court. There was little reason to wait once Jace Orson confessed, which he'd done once the police presented all the evidence they had on him. He was behind the call to her aunt, the hit-and-run and the shooting in front of the restaurant. Most important, he'd admitted to killing Lily.

Chelsea couldn't help wondering how different her life and her father's life would have been if the cops hadn't had tunnel vision seven years earlier. Or if they hadn't accepted Peter's lies. When she thought about it, the anger threatened to consume her, so she tried not to. It worked most of the time.

She tried to stay busy and keep her mind off Travis, too, but that didn't really work, either. She felt as if a part of her was missing. She hadn't realized how deeply she'd fallen for him until he walked away. She wanted to be angry at him, but he'd been honest with her. He told her from the start that he didn't want anything permanent. She was the one who had hoped for more.

But it wasn't to be. She needed to get herself together

and get over him. She repeated that mantra a hundred times a day, but it didn't seem to be working. She still ended every day crying herself to sleep.

Aunt Brenda had demanded that she and Victor appear for family dinner at her house that evening. Her aunt had struggled with the news that she'd been wrong about her brother for so many years. It had taken a few days, but she had finally got up the nerve to call Franklin two days earlier. Chelsea had only been able to hear her aunt's end of the call, and there had been a lot of crying, but it seemed like the siblings wanted to work on building a new relationship.

Aunt Brenda set a big bowl of mashed potatoes on the table and took her seat. She had also cooked a ham, cabbage, homemade biscuits and apple pie for dessert.

"You made a feast, Mom." Victor leaned over and planted a kiss on his mother's cheek.

"Yes, well, we are celebrating." Aunt Brenda beamed. "Franklin is coming home to his family, and it's all Chelsea's doing." Her aunt reached for her hand. "You have grown into an amazing woman, and I could not be prouder of you, sweetie."

"Thank you, Aunt Brenda. And I have an announcement to make, too. We have something else to celebrate. I've decided to go to law school."

Working on her dad's case had shown her just how much she loved helping people and the law. There were too many innocent people in jail. One was too many. And she could do something about it. She'd done her research, and there was still time for her to apply for a spring semester at several area law schools. She could even take a course or two at night as a nonmatriculated student during the fall term and have them count toward her degree when she enrolled as a student.

"Wow, Chels. Congrats," Victor said.

"There are so many people out there who need someone who knows the law to fight for them. I think I can do that for others."

"I know you can," Aunt Brenda said.

"I also spoke to Gerald's estate lawyer," Chelsea went on.

Victor scoffed. "Yeah? I bet Simon was none too pleased to hear they'd reached out to you."

"He was not. It was his job to inform me of the bequest as his father's executor." Chelsea piled mashed potatoes on her plate. "He wanted to get on my good side first."

"Ho ho! That means Gerald must have left you something good."

"Half the estate," Chelsea said.

Her aunt's fork dropped onto her plate with a clang.

Victor's mouth hung open. "Half his estate?"

"Apparently, Gerald wrote the will when Simon and I were married, specifically noting that Simon would take half and I would inherit the other half. He never changed his will. It was why Simon suddenly showed up again and has been calling me."

Victor whooped and raised his water glass with a grin. "Here's to Chelsea becoming an heiress."

"No. I spoke to Simon. I told him that I'd sign over my bequest to him as long as I could keep enough to pay for law school. He was more than happy to accept my proposal."

"Chelsea," Victor groaned.

"It's the right thing to do, Victor. I don't know if Gerald just never got around to changing his will or what, but he meant more to me than money. And I think he'd be happy that I'm going to graduate from law school debt-free. I know I am."

Victor groaned again. "You are too good, cuz."

Aunt Brenda tapped Victor's hand. "There is no such thing as 'too good,' Chelsea has made her decision, and that's that. Now let's eat."

They ate dinner and dessert, and when they were finished, Aunt Brenda insisted on cleaning up everything herself. Victor and Chelsea retired to the living room where Victor pulled up *Iron Man*, her all-time favorite Marvel movie, on Aunt Brenda's television.

"So have you heard from Travis?" Victor asked while the opening credits played.

"No," Chelsea said without looking away from the television. "And I don't expect to." She could feel Victor staring. "I don't. I hired him to do a job, he did it adequately, and now it's over."

"He did it adequately?" Victor's tone was incredulous. He reached for the remote and paused the movie. "It was clear that there was something going on between you two. Now it's just over?" He shook his head. "I don't believe that. You don't do casual relationships."

Chelsea tried forcing back the tears that threatened, but one got away from her.

Victor looked mortified. "Oh, I'm sorry. Don't cry. I shouldn't have brought it up." He wrapped her in a hug.

But it was too late. The floodgates had opened. Chelsea leaned into her cousin's arms. "He didn't want me, Victor. He didn't want me."

TRAVIS SAT AT his desk at the West Security and Investigations office. Phones rang. A meeting was being held in a conference room. Kevin had been holed up in his office all day. It seemed like everyone was busy except Travis.

He hadn't been able to get motivated since he walked out of Chelsea's hospital room and out of her life a week earlier. He needed to shake off his malaise, but all he'd thought about in the last week was Chelsea.

This had never happened to him before. Usually when he ended a relationship, he was able to move on quickly. *Because you never really cared about those women. You never loved them.*

It felt like with each day that passed without Chelsea he hurt even more. Missed her more. He needed to get his head on straight, like Kevin had said.

He glanced over the top of his cubicle wall and saw that his boss's office door was finally open. Thirty seconds later, he knocked on Kevin's door.

Kevin looked away from whatever he'd been reading on his computer monitor.

"Got a minute?" Travis asked.

"Absolutely. What's up?"

Travis crossed to one of the chairs in front of the desk and sat. "I wanted to know if you had anything for me. I'm a little light right now, and you know I like to keep busy."

Kevin's head tilted to the side. "To be honest, I'm surprised you aren't with Chelsea. We can manage around here without you for a few days. You should take some vacation time, you have certainly earned it."

"I don't think that would be a great idea. Chelsea has a lot on her plate right now. Recovering and getting her father out of prison." His gaze slid away from Kevin's face. "Her job is over, so I think it's best we both get on with our lives."

Kevin leaned back in his chair and frowned. "That's what you think is best?"

The pain that had been lingering in Travis's chest for days now became more acute, but he continued to ignore it.

Kevin shook his head, a pitying look on his face. "I thought you were smarter than this."

"Smarter than what?" Travis snapped. "You told me to get my head on straight. It's on straight now."

Kevin looked at him directly. "You think this is what I meant when I told you to get your head on straight? Because right now it looks like you have your head up your—"

Travis growled, cutting him off. "What did you mean then?"

"Man, I can't answer that question for you. Only you can. If you really think letting Chelsea go is the answer, then maybe it is." Kevin shrugged. "Maybe you don't deserve her." he turned back to his monitor. A dismissal.

Travis rose. He made it to the office door. "You really think I could make it work with Chelsea?" he asked, his hand on the doorknob but his back still to Kevin.

"I think when two people want a relationship to work, they make it work. The question is do you want to make it work?"

That was the question.

Chapter Thirty-One

It had been two days since his talk with Kevin, and Travis was no closer to figuring out how to live without Chelsea. He had made a little progress on the professional front, though. Kevin had assigned him to a case that was little more than busywork, collecting files from the Parks and Rec Department. He was heading up the steps of the municipal building when he caught sight of Chelsea's cousin, Victor. He considered turning away to avoid having to make small talk with the man, but Victor's gaze fell on him before he could make his getaway.

The anger marring Victor's face had Travis reconsidering turning and walking away.

Victor increased his pace, coming to a stop in front of Travis. "What the hell did you do to my cousin?"

Travis's heart rate increased. "What are you talking about? Did something happen to Chelsea?" She hadn't called. He'd told her to call if she ever needed anything.

"Yes, something happened to her. You. You happened to her."

Travis's chest tightened even more, but this time from confusion. "I don't understand. Is Chelsea okay?"

"No. She's not okay. She's heartbroken."

He felt himself relax a little, but his chest still felt as if an anvil sat on it. Heartbroken?

"She cried," Victor said, a note of mortification mingling with the anger in his voice. "She cried and said you told her you didn't want her."

"I never said that!"

Victor crossed his arms over his chest. "What did you say then?"

"I—" He hadn't said he didn't want her. He couldn't say that because it wasn't true. But he hadn't told her how much he wanted her, either. He hadn't told her that he loved her. And he did.

He groaned. Kevin was right. His head was up his—

"I told my cousin that if you ever hurt her, you'd be answering to me, and I meant it," Victor said, pulling Travis's attention back to him.

"You're right," Travis responded quickly.

Victor looked at him, confused. "I am? About what?"

"Everything. I'm an idiot. I love your cousin, and I stupidly pushed her away because—"

"Because you're an idiot." Victor grinned.

Travis smiled back. "Yes."

"Good. At least we agree on one thing."

"Look, I need your help."

"Is it helping you make a grand romantic gesture for Chelsea?"

"Let's not get carried away."

Victor tsked. "You are an idiot. If you want to make up with my cousin, you very much need to get carried away. It sounds like you definitely need my help."

CHELSEA PARKED HER car in front of Aunt Brenda's house and got out. The interior of the house was dark, but Victor had called her an hour ago and insisted she meet him there. Since she hadn't been doing much, just rewatching the *Black Panther* movies for the umpteenth time, she'd agreed to. Three more weeks of summer, and then she'd be back at work. The new school year, new students and law classes had to take her mind off Travis, right? She sure hoped so.

She turned her key in the lock on her aunt's door, walked inside and gasped.

A carpet of red rose petals lined the hallway leading to the kitchen.

Was her aunt seeing someone? She would be mortified if Victor called her here to break up his mother's date night.

"Aunt Brenda? It's me, Chelsea."

The voice that called back wasn't her aunt's.

"Chelsea." Travis stepped out of the kitchen, and everything inside her melted. He wore a dark suit and held a dozen red roses in his hand.

"Travis. What are you doing here?"

"I needed to talk to you."

Her heart ached, but she wasn't ready to open it up again and possibly have it shattered further. "About what?"

"About us."

She looked away from him. "There is no us. You made that clear. You don't want me. You have your own life, and I'm not a part of it."

His lips flattened. "You think I don't want you? That's the furthest thing from the truth."

Her eyes met his. "Of course I think that. You left. You walked out on me."

"I was wrong," he said. "I swore to myself I wouldn't let myself love anyone so that I never had to hurt the way

I hurt when I lost my parents and brother. But I hurt her anyway. When I lost you. Worse even because I lost you because I was an idiot."

Chelsea couldn't help it. Hope swelled in her chest. "And you're not an idiot anymore?"

"No. I'm not afraid of being hurt. I'm afraid of living another second without you in my life. I want you, Chelsea. I've never wanted anything more than I have wanted you. And I hope you still want me, too."

Something released inside of her, letting her heartbeat again. She ran into Travis's arms. He held her tightly. Tight enough that she could feel the beating of his heart.

"I love you. Don't you ever leave me again."

"Never again. That's a promise."

Epilogue

Chelsea waited in a private room in the prison family area with her aunt Brenda, Victor and Travis at her side. She'd waited years for this moment, when her father would walk out of prison a free man, but the last two weeks waiting for his release had been some of the longest of her life.

Travis took her shaking hands in his and brought them to his lips.

"I've dreamed about this day for years, and now that it's here I'm so nervous," she said, giving him a small smile.

"That's understandable." He pulled her close and wrapped his arms around her. "You're an amazing woman. I don't know anyone else who would have fought so hard for someone they loved. Your father is lucky to have you." He leaned in close and said in a voice that sent a shiver through her, "I'm lucky to have you." He pressed a kiss to her lips.

They broke apart just as the doors opened.

A pair of guards led her father into the room. He'd changed out of his prison uniform and into the new slacks and cotton pullover that Brenda had bought for her brother.

Chelsea couldn't help the cry that tore from her throat when she saw her father for the first time as a free man. "Dad." She crossed the small room quickly and threw herself into her father's arms.

She felt his tears falling on her shoulder as he squeezed

her tightly. It had been so long since they'd had more than a brief touch. She didn't know if she could bring herself to ever let him go.

But after several minutes, her father stepped back and opened his arms to his sister. Aunt Brenda stepped into her older brother's arms, fat tears sliding down her cheeks.

When she turned, Chelsea noted that Victor was also crying. Even Travis's eyes were red. She stepped back to his side, and his arm slid around her waist.

"Okay, enough with the tears," her father said with the widest smile Chelsea had ever seen on his face. "I've been waiting years to say this. I'm going home!" He kept one arm around his sister and threw the other one around his nephew before heading for the door, laughing.

Chelsea watched her family step out of the room, then looked up into Travis's eyes. "I'm so glad you were here to share this moment with me."

He gazed at her with so much love in his eyes, her breath caught. "I'll always be by your side. There's nowhere else I'd rather be."

* * * * *

You'll find more books in K.D. Richards's West Investigations miniseries, including:

A Stalker's Prey
Silenced Witness
Lakeside Secrets
Under Lock and Key

*Available now wherever
Harlequin Intrigue books are sold!*